The One-Eyed Chevrolet

Stories From Cougar Lake

Kathryn Hartley

Published by Cougar Books, August 2021
ISBN: 978177787250

Typeset: Greg Salisbury
Book Cover Design: Gayll Morrison - www.gayllery.biz
Portrait Photographer: Gayll Morrison - www.gayllery.biz

DEDICATION

This book is dedicated to Larry Kostyniuk.
You left this life too soon and never had a chance
To hold this book in your hands
But you were my first inspiration
And my lifelong fan.
I will always be grateful to you for that.
Sleep well, my friend.

Contents

WELCOME TO COUGAR LAKE

The town of Cougar Lake is like so many small towns sprinkled like grains of cracked black pepper all across the southern latitudes of Canada. They sit on the dusty prairie or nestle at the foot of rolling hills or sit on the shores of quiet lakes. The town of Cougar Lake does all those things.

These towns are so alike a traveler can wonder if he or she actually even left the last one as they roll in off the highway and drive down Main Street. Main Street always looks the same. It may have a different name but it runs straight and true through the heart of the town and sports a diner, a hardware store, a bank, a gas station and a few small shops. The police department is housed in a small, unobtrusive building several blocks off of Main and has room for two desks and a single jail cell. The volunteer fire department will be more prominent and probably built of brick.

The homes are clustered on several surrounding streets with trees in every yard for shade from the summer sun. There might be a small mobile home park toward the outer edges.

Imagine a town of perhaps 1,000 souls nestled in the rolling foothills of southern Alberta just where the prairie climbs to meet the Rocky Mountains. Jeweled lakes support a sudden swath of deciduous trees fringing the edge of the golden prairie and walking up the hills to become the deeper green of evergreens cloaking the lower slopes of the mountains. To the north lies Calgary. To the south is the Montana border; to the west the Stoney Nakoda Nation.

In these towns the people are unique but their lives arise from a common root. Each inhabitant's life and story intersects with others like overlapping circles in the water. Each story stands alone but each story reaches tendrils into others.

In this book the threads holding all the stories together are:

1. Location - the stories are set in the same quintessential small town.
2. Time frame - each story is set in a different month of the year sequentially presented over one and a half years of the life of the town.
3. Characters - as in any small town inhabitants know and interact with and show up in each other's lives.
4. Plus, every once in a while, a classic red 1972 Chevy shows up, even peripherally, in the daily life of the town. Most people know it by sight at least. In a way it captures the spirit of Cougar Lake; maybe a little shabby on the surface but unique, enduring, tough, big hearted and beautiful in its own way.

And so here are just some of the stories, the dramas, the heartbreak and the glories of the town and the people of Cougar Lake.

Chapter 1
The One-Eyed Chevrolet
(September)

In autumn twilight a battered old red Chevy pulled to an abrupt stop at the new traffic light on the corner of Main Street and the highway. The light still wasn't working because the one-man town maintenance crew was busy at his brother's hardware store. Local traffic treated it like the stop sign that had been there for years, pretty much ignoring it, but the out-of-towners slowed things up a bit. Especially the glossy motor homes like the one cruising past.

The driver of the Chev seemed unperturbed by either the delay or the amused glances directed his way by the occupants of the motor home. There were miniature marshmallows still pasted to the windows of his car. On the driver's side the marshmallows spelled out the word M-A-T-T; on the rear window they spelled J-U-S-T-M-A-R-R-I-E-D. The writing on the far window had melted to an unreadable smudge.

As soon as he came to a stop Matt pulled a silver harmonica from his breast pocket and began to play. No sound came through the glass but the tilt of his head and the pleasure on his unshaven face created an illusion of melody. His hair, the dull brown of wet sand, hung in untidy tendrils to the collar of his work shirt. His lower face sprouted shadow and his eyebrows flew up with a slept-in look.

A rusting, yellow pick-up, minus bumpers, pulled up behind the Chevy and blasted its horn. A shaggy, red-blond head emerged through the open window. Matt rolled down his window.

"Hey," said the other man, "I got a bet with Ray says she'll kick you out of bed when you tell her." He grinned, threw the truck in reverse and peeled away in the opposite direction without waiting for an answer. Matt just waved a relaxed hand out the window.

The car ahead of him made its turn onto the highway and drove west toward the mountains. Matt took an extra, careful second to slap the mouth organ clean against his thigh before putting it back in his pocket. He made up for lost time with the speed of his getaway, heading east toward the trailer park.

As he passed the town beach he glanced out at the lake sparkling in the last rays of evening light. On the surface, just past the little island known locally as Three Tree Island for obvious reasons, he could just make out a dark sliver on the water. Probably old Tom Wilkes out fishing in his dilapidated rowboat as usual. At 83 he probably shouldn't be out there alone. His daughter sure worried about him but Matt knew he was a tough old cuss. Matt made a mental note to give Tom a call and invite him out in the motor boat. Although, Matt realized, he hadn't actually seen Tom out and about at all since the previous summer when Matt bought the Chevelle from him. He hoped the old guy was okay.

The trailer park sat just inside the boundary of Cougar Lake Township, about five blocks from the centre of town. Beyond lay scrubby prairie to the east. To the west, beyond the lake, the foothills of Alberta rose like a marching line of dinosaurs against the backdrop of the Rocky Mountains. His trailer faced west toward the mountains and he could just see a glimpse of the lake itself from the bathroom window if he stood on the toilet seat. It wasn't ideal but Matt had plans. He and Nicole would have a place on the lake one day, big enough for kids and maybe his Mom could come and live with them. He knew Jean had to be lonely out there on the farm since his Dad died. He knew she wouldn't be able to manage things much longer out there and he would hate to see his Mom in a senior's home like the one where Nicole worked.

The sun was sliding across the top of the mountains to the west. The lake was already in shadow. He was late.

He pulled the car into the parking area at full speed then jammed on the brake, swinging the wheel hard. The car spun a half circle, sending up dust plumes, and slid to a stop facing back the way it had come. The neighbors, as usual, watched this performance through curtains cautiously twitched aside and eyes wide with concern. Their shiny new Prius was parked as far into their car port as they could get it.

A startled squirrel dashed across the yard, weaving like a silk scarf whipped by a breeze. Then, defying gravity, it flowed up the trunk of the nearest tree and vanished among the almond-tinged leaves.

Matt was out of the car as it skidded to a stop. He tramped around the side of their mobile home and kicked off his steel-toed work boots, letting them drop into the thick carpet of leaves that covered the yard like a rain of gold coins. The bruised leaves gave off a spicy autumn scent. Mud and leaves clung to the boots like a fur coat.

The trailer door slammed shut behind him and was echoed a moment later by the fridge. Cold beer in hand he wandered into the living room and flopped dustily to the sofa. He pulled out the harmonica, downed a third of the beer, then sent his lonely music sliding through the house. He was trying to nail down the notes to Elton John's Candle in the Wind.

After a while he raised his head to call out, "Hey Niki, where are ya? You home?"

"I'm in here," came the reply. "In the bedroom. And don't call me that."

Matt wandered into the bedroom finishing the last of his beer. He put the bottle on the bedside table and wiped his mouth and then his harmonica on the loose tail of his shirt. "Hey," he said. "Sorry I'm a little late home."

Nicole was lying propped up on the bed with her laptop open in front of her. He sat beside her and gently leaned across her for a kiss.

"How you doin', Honey?" he asked.

"I'm fine. Exhausted. I've been on my feet all day."

Matt popped the harmonica in his pocket and reached down to gently massage her feet. She sighed and closed her eyes.

"That feels so good," she said. After a few minutes she gestured with a flick of her finger at the harmonica in his breast pocket. "Why do you have to play that thing so much? I heard you playing it when you came in."

"I don't know. It relaxes me. I like it."

"It drives me crazy."

"I thought… you used to like it," he said, puzzled. "You said you did."

When they were first dating Nicole used to say his playing sounded like the wind singing through the cattails by the lake. He would laugh, embarrassed, but he secretly liked it when she talked in poetry like that.

"Well I don't now," she said. "It makes me sad."

He stared at her. He loved her face with its elegant features, eyes as blue as wild blue flax, dark gold hair illuminated in the last rays or light from the window.

"Well, yeah, it does that to me too, I guess." He paused. "But it's a good kinda sad, don't you think?" He lay down beside her, propped up on one elbow and caressed her dark blonde hair with the other. "It's like the kinda sad you get from memories and old movies and things. Lonely, sort of, but nice. I don't know."

"There's other kinds of lonely that aren't so nice."

"What's that mean?" He ran his hand down her bare thigh but she brushed it roughly away.

"Like this weekend," she said. "You're going hunting with Kenny and Ray this weekend, aren't you? You're going to leave me on my own all weekend. You'd rather be off with those overgrown clowns who'll probably trip and shoot their own feet off, or shoot you."

"Who told you?" he asked, still trying to be cheerful. "We only decided this morning."

"You know how things pass in this town, Matt. Come on, are you really going? Sarah said Ray texted her at lunch and told her to clean up his hunting gear."

"Oh shit. He would. Look, I was gonna tell you..."

"Right. Terrific. It's our one month anniversary, in case you forgot. I thought maybe we might do something really original like be together, God forbid!"

She kicked him to get him off the bed, closed the laptop, then stood and grabbed a hairbrush from the bureau.

"Damn it, Matt, you spent more time with me before we got married. I should have gone to the city on the scholarship instead of taking the job here at the nursing home. Then you and your moronic friends could spend all your time together."

5

"I thought you were working?"

"Jeezus! You just never listen, do you? I told you yesterday I traded shifts so I could have the weekend off."

Matt sat quietly for a moment watching her pull the brush through her hair, then he reached across to touch the soft, tawny waves. She brought the brush down hard against his knuckles.

He flopped back on the bed and listened to the silence stretch between them. He ran his hand through his own scruffy hair and down his cheek, brushing his knuckles against the stubble.

Nicole had campaigned hard against his 'mountain man' look so the day before the wedding, hung over from the stag, he had let Gerry, the barber, shave off his beard. Nicole had tried to get him to cut his hair short, too, but when he came back with just a trim she hadn't kicked up too much fuss. Even so the beard was a loss. The guys had laughed so hard at his naked chin Kenny almost sent the ring rolling down the gutter outside the church.

"The car's running rough again," he said after a few minutes' silence.

"The guys are coming over tomorrow to help me put her up on blocks and we'll take a look at it." He didn't dare say anything about needing to get it running for the weekend. Obviously the weekend was dangerous territory.

"I'm going to have to trash the old girl soon. Soon's we can afford something else."

Nicole still said nothing.

"I guess I oughtta clean her up one of these days, too," he continued. "The damn marshmallows are still stuck on the windows. I wish I knew whose cute idea that was; I'd make the joker clean it off with his tongue."

"Speaking of the wedding..." Nicole slapped the brush onto

the bed, sending a delicate whiff of perfume to him with her movements.

"Yeah?" he said, still staring at the ceiling.

"Why is it before we got married we spent every single weekend together out camping or out at the your Mom's or whatever, but now I see more of Lynn and Sarah than I do my own husband?"

"I thought you liked goin' over to Lynn's on weekends. I thought you girls had a good time together."

"Damn it, Matt! I've told you I hate painting my toenails and exchanging recipes! What's more, I don't think they like it any more than I do. If I want to sit and darn smelly socks or knit baby...well, whatever, which I don't I can do it just as well in front of a tent by the lake. But you didn't even think to ask me did you?"

Matt winced but didn't answer.

"Anyway," she continued. "What's wrong with me going? What am I going to do? Spook the ducks?"

Matt rubbed the back of his hand against the sandpaper of his chin. "Yeah, well...you're all right when you and me go fishing or camping but Niki, that's just us ya know. That's different. I'll have to think about it."

The previous summer they had spent lazy days together, sticky with heat and constant touching. They draped rods over the side of the small fishing boat and listened to the lake's quiet song. At night they curled up in musty sleeping bags zipped together; at dawn they would awaken to see shadows of branches shifting across the canvas tent above their heads and share the bright pine smell in the crisp air as they cooked breakfast over a smoky fire. Afternoons they might explore the length of an icy stream coming in from the mountains; jeans rolled to the knee and beer in a knapsack, just to see if they could find its source.

Then they would sit together against a sap covered trunk and wait for the beer to cool in the water. She loved the feeling of leaning back against his chest while his legs rested on either side of her.

"Well, hand me my jeans while you're thinking," she said. She took the jeans and slipped them on over flowered bikinis.

"Look, Honey, I didn't think you'd want to come. We're goin' for deer this time, ya know."

"What happened to the ducks?" she asked, sucking in her breath to zip the jeans. "They all fly south? Or are they just in hiding? I wouldn't blame them."

"Kenny and I got our bag limits already," Matt said, ignoring her snide tone. Nicole didn't prompt him further but stood, hands on hips, watching him pull nervously at the threads in the checkerboard quilt: a wedding gift from his mother, Jean.

"Babe," he said. "It's just that I know how you feel about hunting. You still don't understand what I get out of it. With big game especially it's great; just you and that big buck and one of you's got to be better than the other. You're damn proud when it's you, see? Besides, I don't think the guys would be thrilled to have someone along who…"

"Yeah, I know. We've been over it before." Nicole picked up a jar of Peach Blush from the bureau and pushed her hair back from a thin forehead to peer into the mirror. "What difference does it make how I feel about the murder of helpless…okay, okay, I'm sorry." She wiped a trace of the greasy makeup from her fingers onto her jeans then came and sat beside him on the sagging, second-hand mattress.

"Look, I won't say anything wrong, promise. And I don't need to go out with a gun myself so they don't have to worry about getting shot in the back, and you've said before you don't expect me to do any of the skinning and gutting."

"Then I don't get it. What d'you want to come for?"

"Matt, I love being outdoors, you know that! And I got married to be with you! What's wrong with that? Besides, when you do shoot your foot off I'll be there to put a Bandaid on it." Nicole didn't smile but there was the slightest amused lift to one eyebrow above one of her blue eyes. Matt laughed and reached for her hand, crushing her fingers in what was supposed to be an affectionate squeeze. His blunt fingernails were cracked in places halfway down their length and his hands dry-roughened from his work at the cement plant in Exshaw.

"The other wives won't want to come," he said, half thoughtful, half hopeful. "They'll probably spend the weekend in Calgary at Costco."

"I don't care what the other wives do! You think the minute I said 'I do' I should have become just like every other wife and mother in town; sit patiently at home waiting to cook whatever the mighty hunter caught? If the other wives had always gone do you think for a minute you'd want me staying home even if I wanted to?" She got up and began angrily gathering loose hangers from the closet floor. "Why do you have to be such a follower?!"

Matt watched her carefully for a moment.

"I'm not like that, Niki. You know I'm not." He kept his voice gentle. "You sure you wanna come?"

"Yes!"

He lay back against the pillow and smiled then, reaching an arm toward her. She came, slipping out of her sandals, leaving them trailing like footprints across the rug. She stretched out on top of him, nibbling at his pouting lower lip.

He tried to roll them over in formation but she resisted so they lay side by side in compromise. Her jeans were tight and had a zipper that viciously resisted opening so he gave up and lifted her T shirt instead, drifting a line of scratchy kisses across her stomach, leaving pink streaks against the pale skin. She had once left crimson tooth marks on the base of his neck and he had worn the same turtleneck sweater for a week, but marks of love didn't seem to bother her. She ran her hands through his dusty hair.

"I'll ask the guys," he said.

She froze for a second then rolled away and off the bed. "Why?!"

"Because you said...?"

"No, I mean why do you have to ask their permission?"

Matt reached for her again but she backed against the bureau, glaring at him. "Look," he sighed, unbuttoning his shirt, "They got a say in any plan changes, okay? That's just the way it is."

He threw his shirt on the bed. "I'll ask!"

He walked into the bathroom, dropping his belt and jeans in a noisy heap on the floor. The thunder of the shower soon absorbed any sound from the other room. He turned his face into the hot spray and his hair went from dull to glossy as the concrete dust whirled away down the drain.

With a finger he drew a stag's head in the film of steam on the shower doors then, with one sweep of his hand, he turned the deer into a colourless rainbow. "Gotcha," he muttered.

There was nothing more said until Friday afternoon when the minimally repaired Chevy discharged three men in dusty clothes and three cold beers were brought out to the lawn chairs in the yard. Kenny, Matt's best man, was a strawberry blond with a cheerfully florid complexion and a loud, easy manner that was endearing until he was crossed. His sulks were legendary and long.

Ray was more like Matt: a little quiet, a little thoughtful but always ready for fun. He was the one who came up with the pranks, Matt would work out the logistics, Kenny would execute. It was teamwork left over from grade school.

Matt's attempts to get a confession from Ray on the matter of marshmallows had so far been fruitless.

"Look, you jerk," he complained cheerfully as they sat in the golden September sun. "Nobody else could come up with something like that. Admit it. Tin cans are the best the rest of them could do. Or molasses in the bed. No, the marshmallows, that was a stroke of genius."

Ray laughed, "Yeah, that was pretty good, wasn't it?" He looked across the cattails in the distance. "Wish I'd thought of it," he said innocently.

"Ah shit, you know you did. Come on, say it."

"Hey, flattering my brilliance won't get a confession outta me. Good try but no cigar, chum."

"You guys are gonna lick those things off, so help me."

Kenny sputtered, "I didn't have..."

Nicole came out just then, letting the screen door slam behind her. Her slim figure moved gracefully across the lawn on strong legs. Her work involved a good deal of walking and lifting so she was fit without having to try.

"Hey, Nik," Ray called. "Hear you wanna come bag a deer with us, that right?"

Matt pulled out his harmonica and began picking out the notes to 'Summertime'. The oldies were always easier to play.

"It's Nicole," Nicole said, coming over to stand behind Matt's chair with her fingers spread across his chest and her chin resting on the top of his head.

"Everybody on a hunt has to do their share, ya know," said Kenny. "And us guys share everything out in the woods." He grinned, looking down the line of her denim hips. "Don't we Matt?"

At this he and Ray looked at each other and laughed with the uncertain bravado of schoolboys expecting trouble. Matt swung a good natured kick at the nearest friend.

"So what's the vote, guys?" he asked.

"I don't want a woman walking around the same woods as me with a rifle. I'm not that crazy," Ray said.

"Me neither," added Kenny.

"You're just afraid of having a 'woman' see you make idiots of yourselves out there, that's all," Nicole said with a tight smile. "I promise I won't tell a soul what I see."

"What d'you want to tag along for anyway?" Kenny asked.

"It's not for your scintillating company, I assure you," she snapped.

Kenny looked baffled.

"C'mon, Nik. Women don't go hunting," Ray said with a smirk. "Hand a woman a gun, she'd pee her pants." They all laughed, even Matt. Nicole glared down at him.

"You… are jerks!" Nicole said in a precise, cold voice. "All of you!"

"Ah, come on, Babe." Matt grabbed her hands. "They're only kidding."

Kenny snorted. Nicole didn't wait for more. She pulled away from Matt, churning up small whirlpools of leaves as she marched, rigid with anger, back to the trailer.

"Oops," said Ray.

Matt watched her go, his face uncertain. He turned to Kenny who opened his mouth to speak...and left it open, staring over Matt's shoulder. Matt spun around.

Nicole stood in the doorway with his Remington 308

cradled in her arms; her face rigid with anger. Silently she moved toward them.

"Hey, hey, hey, Niki..." he started to rise from his chair. Nicole remained silent. She looked around carefully then swung the rifle into position against her shoulder.

"Easy! Easy! What are you doing?" Matt yelled, turning slightly pale.

Nicole released the safety and pulled back the bolt with a sharp click.

"Holy Shit! She's gonna kill us!" yelled Ray, diving out of his chair into a shower of gold leaves. Kenny tried to back up while half sitting, half standing. The chair fell backwards and he went with it but there was not a breath of laughter.

"Left headlight at 40 yards," Nicole said in icy tones. She sighted down the road to the pull-off where Matt always parked the car.

"Nicole, don't do anything st..." Matt yelled, forgetting all endearments. Then the crack of the rifle was followed by the crash of glass and the whunk of metal against metal. He ducked. When the shot echoed away across town he cautiously opened his eyes to see Nicole standing still, staring at the car. The Remington had absorbed most of the recoil but the report had been momentarily deafening. She recovered slowly, the grim look of determination returning to her face.

"You," she said, pointing at Matt, "Should have remembered! I told you I went with Dad every year. I told you that!" She snapped the safety back on and stalked back into the trailer.

Only then did Matt turn to survey the damage. He walked down to the Chevy and bent to brush glass from the bumper.

"Holy Shit!" said Ray again, coming up behind him. Matt stood and put a finger in a new hole in the fender where the bullet had exited after shattering the headlight.

"Hit the rad?" called Kenny from where he was struggling with his chair which appeared to have him trapped.

"Nah," Ray called back. "Bull's-eye on the headlight though."

Matt let out his breath in a long, low whistle as if coming out of a dream. "Did you see that?" he exclaimed as Kenny finally joined them.

"Couldn't miss it, could I?" Kenny grumbled, pulling leaves from under his shirt. The three stood back and stared at the crippled car. Kenny and Ray glanced at each other and began to smirk.

"Hot damn!" Matt whispered, still dreaming. Then he looked at his friends, "Did you see that?!" Suddenly he punched Kenny with a quick right and a left to the shoulder then danced over and took a swipe at Ray. "God Damn!" he yelled, a ragged smile breaking through the shadowed half of his face.

"You know," Ray said, "She just might have done you a favour. Now maybe you'll get rid of this hunk of junk."

❧

Next morning when the mist lay still as milk over the valley a red Chevy Chevelle pulled up to the traffic light at Main and the highway, its single headlight shining gold in the cool dawn light. Its windows reflected the pale silver morning.

"Is this junk heap gonna even make it to camp?" grumbled a voice from the back seat.

Matt smiled. "C'mon man. She may be old but she's got heart."

The old car didn't even pause before squealing onto the highway and heading for the low, wooded foothills to the west.

"You guys aren't going to get a chance to shoot each other;

Matt's going to kill us all first," Nicole groaned as she slapped Matt's thigh in mock anger. "And I don't know about you guys but I have to be back at work next week. My patients need me."

A voice from the back seat said, "Never mind him, Annie Oakley. Just navigate this one-eyed beast in the direction of the nearest Starbucks. We gotta get us a couple of gallons of hot coffee back here or the deer won't have a thing to worry about from us."

Matt just laughed. Guiding the wheel with one hand he cupped the other around his silver harmonica and put it to his lips.

Chapter 2
Hike To Tomorrow
(October)

Megan Towers jabbed her hiking stick firmly into the ground with each step, sliding a bit in the wet leaves on the trail. Grey-blue light filtered through the sparse trees and did little to warm the late October chill. Clouds tumbled across the sky in the cold wind. Their shadows scampered off the slopes of the mountains.

The parking lot disappeared behind her as the trail opened up toward the silver lake.

She had never expected to be back in Cougar Lake for any other purpose than to visit her parents. Yet here she was substitute teaching at the high school for a teacher on pregnancy leave. She had been looking forward to spending some time today with her friend, Nicole. They planned to hike the trail around Cougar Lake then go to the Copper Kettle for lunch. But Nicole had called to say she was feeling very sick this morning.

"You're probably exhausted. That's 6 days straight you've worked, isn't it? Are you going to be okay?" Megan asked.

"I'll be fine. You're probably right; I just feel really tired and overwhelmed right now. Plus Matt's Chevy has some sort of problem, again! I wish he would get rid of that thing. So anyway he took my jeep to work today. Do you want to try again for tomorrow?"

"I have to work tomorrow, Nicole. Sorry." Megan felt the grey empty sensation again, the one she had been having almost daily lately. She shook her head and smoothed a hand across the back of her neck.

"Right. Of course I knew that, Megan. Sorry. Listen, Matt will be away hunting this weekend and I'm too tired to go with him this time. Why don't you come over here? We'll have dinner on the deck and have a good talk. I know you have stuff that's sitting on your chest, Girlfriend, and I think you need a chance to work it through. I can be a good listener you know?"

Megan laughed. Nicole had always been a sympathetic ear, which is probably what made her so good at her job working with the seniors at the care home. They so often just needed someone to talk to. Just like the kids she taught at the high school. Some of them came from pretty difficult home environments and having a trusted teacher to talk to sometimes made all the difference.

"You know what? That would be great. I think I'll do the hike this morning anyway. I'm feeling restless. I'll see you on the weekend then. I'll bring the wine."

"See you then. Take care." Nicole rang off.

On her first day back in her old hometown Megan had gotten together with Nicole for coffee and muffins then they went out to visit Nicole's father's memorial bench. It sat at the edge of the cemetery grounds looking out over the lake. Nicole ran her hands gently over the engraved plaque on the back of the bench then they sat together and got caught up on what had been happening in their respective lives. Nicole was particularly frustrated with the constraints of small town life and Megan was hard pressed not to say, I told you so. But she thought it.

The two young women had been close friends growing up.

Their parents had been good friends, too. But Megan had been the restless soul who needed more challenge and she was the one who left for Edmonton right after graduation. They kept in touch by email mostly, plus the occasional phone call. Nicole had settled into married life with Matt and her work at the senior's home, although in the past year there had been a thread of discontent weaving its way into a lot of their conversations.

This morning, she thought she detected a note of frustration again in Nicole's voice. Maybe after her walk she would swing by and take her friend a tall cappuccino from the Copper Kettle.

The trail opened up near the shoreline. The weak sun shone on water speckled with small clusters of migrating Bufflehead and Blue Winged Teal. Megan stood near the shallows gazing at the familiar crest of tree-covered mountains across the lake. A few golden leaves still clung tenaciously to branches but most trees were already bare. Only the spikes of evergreens gave colour to the blue-grey ridge of the distant Rocky Mountains.

The wind was cooler than she had expected when she set out this morning. It swept strong across the water one moment and died to a whisper the next. In the process it had shredded the morning mist to rags. Above her the tops of the trees swayed in the wind. From across the lake came the sound of a Winter Wren. The camel-hump hills layered into the distance.

Her parents loved to hike, kayak, canoe, birdwatch. You name it; they did it. Cougar Lake was perfect for them. It hadn't really rubbed off all that much. Yes, she still went out for walks in the woods. A person needed to get some fresh air and exercise somehow. Nicole, too, had always been seriously into the outdoors and she had the long, lean, blond looks to go with it.

Megan was chunky, solid, and barely 5'4". Her dark brown hair frizzed if she didn't keep it short. She had admitted to herself long ago that envy coloured their friendship a bit but now she found that their lives had moved into such different spheres the feeling was more one of admiration.

Nicole had managed to make a solid life here with her husband and she appeared to fit well into the small town life. Megan had no interest in living here again but coming to visit felt comforting.

She left the water and headed up the trail to where it bent and began to climb. She would only go as far as the rock outcrop where they used to have bonfire parties, rest there a bit, and then get back to her parent's house. At 28 she found living with them again a bit constricting. But she was only staying until this assignment was over. There was hardly any point renting when she would be heading back to Edmonton in a few months, hopefully to a full time position at a school there.

She felt the grey emptiness churn up from her stomach again. What the heck was that? Maybe she hadn't eaten enough for breakfast. Yes, that was all it was.

Her feet slipped on the soggy ground and she dug her hiking stick in harder, putting more weight on the stick. Her breathing sounded rough and hollow in her ears as she inhaled the crisp oxygen-laden air. She had to admit the clean air and quiet spaces of Cougar Lake were a huge improvement over Edmonton. It was a nice city but it was a city nonetheless.

Someday she would travel, maybe get married. Probably not have kids though. Teaching gave her enough of that every day. She had plans. If she could just start saving up to make some of them happen. That was the problem. Until she had a full time position how was she ever supposed to put away any savings to do these things?

Her nose ran from the cold. She stopped, dug out a Kleenex, blew her nose more violently than necessary. She took a final wipe with the Kleenex and lifted her gaze. Every muscle in her body froze in terror. She was looking straight into the cold, golden eyes of a cougar.

The cat was motionless. It sat sphinxlike on a rock 30 feet above her to the left of the trail. If she hadn't stopped at that exact spot she would never have seen it.

Fear ripped through her. It felt like acid being shot through her veins. She couldn't move. The eyes stared straight at her without a flicker of movement. She had never seen anything so menacing and cold. She knew, and she knew the cat knew, that she was utterly helpless. The advice always said not to run from a cougar but it was irrelevant. Her feet and legs were encased in solid stone. They wouldn't have moved if she wanted them to.

Kleenex still pressed to her face, she waited for the enormous cat to leap. Her life was over. There was no doubt. She had always known, of course, that her life would end someday but someday had always seemed so very, very far in the future. To find her death staring at her now, today, with such menace was beyond her worst nightmare.

She could only see the cougar's face, paws and shoulders; those powerful, tawny shoulders that any moment would propel that cat toward her, probably no more than three bounds. For the briefest moment she imagined how it was going to feel when the claws and teeth ripped her apart.

She whimpered. She couldn't help it. The cat's ears twitched forward. She slowly lowered the Kleenex from her face, took her last deep breath. Even knowing it was utterly hopeless, she forced one foot a fraction of an inch backward. The other foot followed.

The monstrous paws flexed on the ledge of rock. The tawny cat's shoulders rocked back and forth. The tip of its tail twitched.

Then it leapt. It dropped to the trail in front of her. Its

muscles bunched, ready for the next spring. Megan screamed. Its front paws slammed violently back and forth against the ground sending up a spray of leaves. Amber eyes flashed. It snarled.

Megan stumbled backwards. "NO, no, no, no!"

The big cat crept another step closer.

"I don't want to die," she said to the cougar. Her voice choked in her throat. She held her hand out palm up. "Please don't! Please. I haven't lived yet."

The rounded ears twitched forward as the cat took another step, then crouched. It stared unblinking.

Megan forced her feet to take another step back. She fought the desperate urge to turn and run.

"I don't want to die," she repeated. Then she screamed to the heavens with grief for all those lost years her future would have held. She raised her fists in the air.

"I DON'T WANT TO DIE!" Her voice shattered the very air in the forest. Her throat felt shredded from the force of her screams.

For a split second she saw a startled expression widen those icy golden eyes. The cougar raised its body from the crouch, ready to take the last leap to cover the ground between them.

She screamed again, wordlessly this time, and covered her face with her hands. She couldn't bear to watch death come. Warm urine ran down her legs. The Kleenex dropped from her nerveless hands and drifted to the wet ground.

A Chickadee called from a nearby branch. Golden leaves whispered in a gust of wind. The last sounds she would ever hear. Then silence.

Megan forced her reluctant eyes to open, terrified of what she might see. Her hands trembled violently in front of her face. She lowered them. The trail in front of her was empty.

The rock above was empty. She whirled around to look behind her. Nothing.

She flung her stick into the woods, turned and ran back down the trail. Sliding, falling, pounding, breathing, whipped by branches, heedless of everything, she ran.

Her borrowed car, parked at the trail head parking lot, appeared as a haven, a miracle. She slammed the doors and locked them. Her body was trembling so violently she could do nothing but sit there, gasping for breath, tears pouring down her neck and into her collar. She shivered and cried until she was too exhausted to continue.

The smell of cold urine filtered through her consciousness. "Oh God," she muttered. Gingerly she took the plastic bag, supplied by the rental company for use as a garbage bag, and slipped it underneath her to try to keep the wet from soaking into the seat. Too late. She knew that immediately.

"I'll have to shampoo it before I take it back," she thought. Then she burst into fresh tears at the realization that she was still alive to be able to worry about such things as a wet car seat.

She forced her fingers, finally, to turn the key. The car started but she couldn't remember how to drive. Every thought, every detail of her life, had been wiped away and all that remained was the silence of the forest, the cold of the snow, and the tawny eyes of death.

Eventually Megan found her way to town.

"Hello dear," Dara said as she came in. "How was your walk?"

"Mum, I... " Megan croaked.

"Oh, Honey. What happened? You sound like you have a really bad cold. Is your throat sore?"

"Yes, my throat's sore but..."

"Well, why don't you go on up and get into a nice hot bath. I'll bring up some honey lemon tea."

It had been more than a decade since Megan had felt the need for someone to care for her. It felt wonderful.

"Thanks Mum," she croaked, and went to do as she was told, all her own will, resentment, and independence leeched from her like a toothpaste tube emptied and flat. As the tub with filling she put her wet slacks into the washing machine and filled it with cold water. Her mother did not have to know about that.

A hot bath, a cup of tea did help tremendously. She came downstairs in her bathrobe and slippers.

"Come and tell me what's wrong, Honey," her mother said. "You look like you've seen the proverbial ghost."

A shaky smile quivered across her lips. "I almost was one," she said.

She told Dara about the encounter with the cougar but once she started talking the floodgates wouldn't close.

"If I had died today, Mum, what has my life been worth?"

Dara put a hand over her mouth and tears welled in her eyes.

"I don't mean to you and Dad, Mum. I mean to the world. What have I accomplished? I've had a few boyfriends but no one special. I've got my teaching degree. Fat lot of good that's done me so far. No family of my own, no house, no passionate hobbies. What am I doing?"

She paused to sip her tea.

"Honey, you've done so much. Just to get your degree is a huge accomplishment. You've got family and friends. And you know you have a home here whenever you want to come back."

"I know, Mum. But speaking of friends, look at Nicole as an example. She has a good husband, a home, a job where she makes a real difference to people. Sometimes I think she buried herself in a backwoods town but the old people she cares for seem to sincerely love her and thrive under her care. She matters to them. I went into teaching because I thought I could make a difference as a teacher. I wanted to guide fresh young minds into a love of learning. It's not turning out that way. I can't land a permanent position. My stints as a temp feel like glorified babysitting. If I had died today nothing would be better for me having been on the planet."

She looked up to see her mother glaring at her.

"Darling girl, you can just stop feeling sorry for yourself right now. You have a wonderful mind, a warm heart that's just a little lost right now, a loving family, friends, a good education, health, and all the opportunities in the world. You have absolutely no right to be feeling sorry for yourself."

She took Megan's empty teacup from her hand. "Now, you go on up to bed and have a good sleep. I happen to know you sleep like a Mexican jumping bean. That's no kind of rest. I'll call you when supper's ready. And if you don't sleep and you just lie there counting your blessings, well that won't hurt either."

Megan slept straight through for the next 24 hours. Never in her life had she done that. But then again, never in her life had she been so close to death.

Slowly waking to the half-light of a grey October afternoon she thought about the fact that she should be dead right now.

Nicole was horrified when she told her about the encounter as they shared a bottle of wine on Saturday. Even in the trailer park all the homes were already festooned with pumpkins, ghosts, witches and spiders in preparation for Halloween. There were lots of families with young children in this area of town so the residents went all out.

"I've never even see one," Nicole said, staring at Megan.

"Well I wish I hadn't. Do you think it was a wakeup call? I mean, I'm kind of in this limbo in my life. Maybe it was the universe telling me life is short, get on with it?"

When Nicole didn't answer Megan looked up at her. Her lips were pressed together in an effort to smother laughter.

"I'm sorry, honey," Nicole spluttered. "But no. It was a goddam cat. Not the Arch Angel Gabriel."

Megan began to laugh as well. "I never did like cats," she said. And at that the two girls burst into laughter.

When their laughter subsided Nicole said, "Seriously though Megan, if you decide to take a different direction, I wish you joy in whatever decision you make but I will miss you."

They touched their wine glasses together with a sound like the ringing of fairy bells.

ॐ

Two days later Mega sat in the kitchen watching Dara bake a raspberry pie.

"I'm quitting my job, Mum," she said. As the words left her mouth a flock of butterflies went mad in her belly. Was she really doing this? Safe, sensible Megan? "I'll finish out this assignment to the end of November then I'll go back to Edmonton and give my notice."

Her mother dropped the rolling pin and put flour dusted hands to her hips.

"Why on earth would you do that, dear?"

"I'm never going to get a permanent placement. I know teachers with more seniority than me who are still subbing. There's so much more I want to do with my life." She hugged her arms across her chest trying to soothe the butterflies. "I'm scared about it, Mum. I admit that, but honestly if I'm going to follow a dream it has to be now, right?"

"But dear, how will you live?"

"I'll find a way. I'll go to Thailand and teach English. I'll learn to scuba dive and use my RRSP's to buy a dive boat and start a charter. I could move to Oregon and get a job in a hotel on the seashore. There's a million things I could do but I need to just do them. I want to be 105 years old and sit in my wheelchair in the sun and treasure my memories like those old folks Nicole takes care of every day. I want to be able to say I had a hell of a good life. That's what I want."

An image rose in her mind. She stood at the edge of the dock. She was 12 years old. The water beckoned. The summer sunlight buttered the surface of the lake to smooth gold. Kids ran from the far end of the dock, flashed past her, and leapt into the water with a yell of pure joy. She stood there shivering, then turned and walked back to the safety of the beach where her parents read in their beach chairs. She sat and watched silently as the other children sent glistening sprays of water into the blue air, yelling and laughing.

Her mother wiped her hands on a towel and came and sat down. She took Megan's hands in both of hers.

"Well, my sweet baby girl, if that's what you want then you go for it. What I've discovered is that tomorrow becomes yesterday pretty darn quick and then it's gone. What can I do to help?"

❧

Dara dropped her daughter at the Greyhound station on the last weekend of November. The town was veiled in drifting snow.

Even so, the temperature was mild enough that they drove the short stretch of highway into town with the windows open and snowflakes gently floating in. They skirted the edge of the lake, came to a stop at the new traffic light, then drove two more blocks to the station.

"Have you got everything?" Dara asked her daughter as she helped her unload a suitcase and sleek leather laptop bag from the trunk.

"Got everything I came with this time, Mum." On Megan's last visit, two years ago, she had been in such a rush to leave that she had left several articles of clothing and a school text in the guest room. The clothing was still waiting for her when she arrived this time but the text had been essential for teaching her fall classes that year so her mother had to ship it to her by Express Post.

"I really hope you can find your way, Sweetheart."

"Well I can't get very lost on a Greyhound bus from Cougar Lake to Edmonton, Mum, can I?"

"That isn't what I meant and you know it."

Dara gathered her daughter in a tight hug and held her there for a moment. The two women were almost the same height and build: short and solid with almost no waistline. They looked like sisters except Dara's brown hair was starting to show silver strands at the temples; Megan's was still a rich, chocolate brown.

"I know what you mean, Mum. I'm going back to Edmonton and officially quit my job then I'll take time off to do some research but I'm pretty sure I will be travelling come spring. I'll let you and Dad know where I am and what I'm doing, okay? Listen, say bye to Nicole and Matt for me will you. I didn't get a chance to see much of them this time."

"I will. I'll be seeing Matt's mother tomorrow as a matter of fact. We both still volunteer every year to help with the Harvest

Market." You're going to miss the fun, you know. You couldn't stay one more day?"

"No, they're expecting me at work Monday. I'm glad you're still involved."

Megan put her cases beside a battered bench just outside the Greyhound station door. She watched the snow settling onto the cracked concrete of the parking area. Every few minutes the glass door opened and someone would come in or out surrounded by a cloud of steamy air that smelled faintly of human sweat and gasoline. Bus station odor.

"Sometimes we need a wakeup call to come to our senses, Mum, don't we."

"We do indeed. We need to be shaken out of complacency, sometimes forcibly."

Just inside the open bus barn door, a sleek, caramel cat stared at them with a distinctly unwelcoming glare. Megan shivered.

"Are you cold, Dear?"

"No, I'm fine." Her mother's solicitous caregiving used to annoy Megan but it seemed comforting now; something she did not have in her life in Edmonton where she lived alone. She had a nice apartment in the Woodlands area in the northwest with a great view out over the park but it was such a sterile life she was looking forward to the excitement of the trip she was already planning to take as soon as she gave notice. She hadn't said as much to her parents for fear of the shock on their faces but she had been on the internet for the last few days and was seriously considering a position teaching English as a second language in Thailand.

A loud rumble and a hiss of brakes announced the arrival of the bus.

"Bye, Mum. And thanks for everything." She hugged her

mother one more time, turning away from the tears she saw forming in her mother's eyes.

"Goodbye, Dear. Safe journey." Her mother's choked voice followed her up the bus stairs. As the Greyhound exhaled heavily and pulled away, she stared out the window at the snow covered streets. It looked just like every other small town she had ever seen or even read about. One long main street which, in Cougar Lake, was even called Main Street. Narrow store fronts facing each other, competing for the attention of the few slow moving shoppers who were out on a snowy late November day. Probably buying a new farm gadget at the hardware store, she thought. Her cynicism about small town life had tempered a bit this last visit but she still had to be careful to keep snide comments to herself.

She sighed and settled back into her chair as she left Cougar Lake behind. She looked out over the spreading valley. In Calgary she would connect with a north bound bus to Edmonton. From there…she didn't know yet but it would be a new horizon.

Chapter 3
The Woman Who Said No
(November)

Lisa Campbell carefully hung her apron in the back room and walked out through the café, shrugging her coat on. She gave a small wave to one of her regulars, picked up her tips from the cashier and went out into the cold November afternoon.

The Copper Kettle sat tightly wedged between the laundromat and the town's only pharmacy. The decorative wooden scroll work across the top edge of each business was identical but painted pine green, copper, and fuchsia respectively. The doors were all the same squared off shape with push bar handles. When a customer walked into the restaurant the whiff of chemicals from the laundromat followed them in for a moment before being drowned by the smell of freshly brewed coffee, bacon and french fries. The Kettle wasn't fancy but it was still the most popular place to eat in town. The only other choices were a few coffee shops and the dining room at the Cougar Lake Hotel.

Lisa had waitressed there part time for as long as she could remember, probably 25 years or more now. There was a comfort in the familiar and she had no desire to do anything else. So why on earth she had decided to do something so out of character as to have her hair cut, she couldn't understand.

She stood for a moment with her hand on the door of the hair salon. She could just go home. Call them and tell them she was sick. Her sister's comment on the phone last week still rang in her ears.

"It makes you look old, Lisa. Greying hair hanging to your shoulders. I know you've always worn it long but really, it's just not attractive anymore."

She took a deep breath of damp, icy air and pushed the door open.

When Lisa left an hour later she felt truly sick and it wasn't just the odors of hair dyes and heavily perfumed shampoos she'd been breathing. It was the sight of her autumn brown hair shot with silver lying on the salon floor. It made her dizzy and tears pricked at the corners of her eyes.

It frightened her to see a stranger staring back from the mirror. It wasn't what she had wanted at all, of course. She had known it wouldn't be.

"Just a little off," she had said. "Just to tidy it up." She had cut her own and Patrick's hair all their married life. Always exactly the same way. But this….this was not her. The grey was far more pronounced and the short layers made her look like a pixie in a windstorm.

"You look great," the hairdresser said as she whipped off the cape. "That tousled style is way more up to date." The young woman's dark purple nails flashed as she accepted Lisa's money.

"Yes. Of course," Lisa whispered. "Thank you." She avoided looking in the mirror again and instead watched the hairdresser's heavily jewelled fingers close over the bills. Her bright smile followed Lisa out the door.

Why, when she had to deal with young people like that, did she feel 75 instead of 55? Even when she had been that age she had never been the confident, glittering flower these girls were.

Lisa stood for a moment on Main Street to button her coat. Her dark brown coat was fraying at the edges of the pockets and around the button holes a bit. She faced into the cold wind and let it flatten the hair away from her face before she pulled her knitted wool cap down tightly over the new hairdo.

She should have been home at their apartment long ago. Her intention had been to pop into the hairdressers around the corner after work, get a little trim, and still be home before him. But now Patrick would hit the roof when he saw this short, choppy style. If he saw it, she corrected herself.

A single star shone in the cobalt blue of the early evening sky. She lifted the collar of her coat up around her chin. Her thin neck and protruding collar bones were always cold. She put her head down into the wind that blew in from the lake and began the long walk home to the apartment.

As soon as she got there she would wash out the wildness. Maybe Patrick wouldn't notice and there wouldn't have to be a fight about the wasted money. And maybe he still wouldn't be home. Lisa felt a hot sense of anxiety. If he was home and he yelled at her, swore, even threw things, at least it would break up the painful silence of the apartment.

It had been 4 days now. Even on a bender he didn't usually stay away this long. And the rent was due. Why hadn't she gone straight home after work? She should have been there when he got home! She started to run, stumbling in her thick-soled work shoes. She passed the Legion Hall where he usually drank. She didn't dare even turn her head. As she crossed Main Street an old red sports car with a broken headlight honked at her as it zipped past. She scuttled guiltily onto the sidewalk.

Her flagging footsteps veered up the side street to their apartment block. In the lobby she fumbled for her keys, dropped them, and blushed for no one.

"Mrs. Campbell!" The female voice coming from the first floor apartment was sour with disapproval. "I've been meaning to come up and see you. Your rent's way past due, you know."

"I know, Mrs. Baker," Lisa said. "I'm terribly sorry. Patrick will be down with the rent first thing tomorrow morning, if that's all right? You see the company sends his cheques from…" Strange, her voice kept slipping away, choking her.

"I wish," interrupted the landlady, "You people would realize I have bills too and I can't pay them with excuses." She stood at the second floor railing and glared down at Lisa. The landlady looked soft and round like a baked apple but her voice, and her attitude, more closely resembled razor blades.

"Yes. I know. I'm so sorry. I promise Patrick will…"

"Well you see that he does!" Mrs. Baker snapped her jaw shut and slammed indignantly back into her apartment.

Lisa knew perfectly well she shouldn't have promised any such thing. Who knew if Patrick would be home tomorrow? What on earth was she going to do?

Stairs repeated themselves, line by line, in front of her as she climbed. The echo of her footsteps rebounded from wall to wall up the narrow stairwell. When she stepped into her apartment the silence was like a thousand pillows locking her inside her head.

"Patrick?"

The damp chill in the empty apartment smelled faintly of old cooking smells. The darkness seeped in through the single pane front window. It all felt overwhelmingly lonely.

The only person she could think of to talk to was her upstairs neighbour, Angela Leland. Angela had a lot of qualities in common with Patrick; always knew what to do, what was best for everyone and told them so. Still, Lisa found her reassuring to be with. She and Patrick hated each other. Which might just be the best antidote right now.

The odor of fried onions seeped through the hallways and followed her up the stairs. She tapped gently on Angela's door then used her foot to smooth down bumps in the old, grey carpet while she waited.

"Lisa!" Angela exclaimed when she opened the door. "What's wrong? What's that bastard done now?"

Lisa glanced quickly up and down the hall; sure that everyone on the floor had heard her. Angela's voice always made Lisa wince. Her neighbour stood 5'8", a good 3" taller than Lisa herself. Her well-muscled body gave her the smooth, clean movements of an athlete. Her mane of black hair and hawk-sharp features punctuated the contrast between the two women. Lisa was always painfully conscious of her own bland appearance: her mousy hair, her bony frame and her pale, indoor skin.

"I…" Lisa choked. "Patrick…he's gone."

"For good this time?"

She nodded miserably. "I think so."

It was hard enough to face it inside but to admit to someone else that her husband had left her was humiliating. She felt a sudden strangling terror. She was about to turn and run when Angela grasped her arm and hooted, "Well c'mon in, Honey. We'll celebrate!"

When Lisa left several hours later she felt drained from crying at Angela's kitchen table but her tears were dry now. Angela was comforting in a gritty sort of way. Nothing frightened or slowed that woman and it was hard to remember to be frightened when she was around.

Lisa's fingers tightened around the scrap of paper Angela

had given her along with strict instructions to see the man whose name was written on the scrap.

"He's one of the few lawyers we have here in town but he is also the best at dealing with deadbeat husbands. Believe me, I know. You're gonna need somebody to help you get sorted legally and you're gonna need support money. Is Mrs. B on at you about the rent?"

Angela knew about Patrick drinking up the rent money. Everyone in the building knew.

Lisa nodded.

"Tell you what," Angela continued. "You're on late shift tomorrow, right?" She didn't wait for an answer. "We'll go together in the morning. I can introduce you and help get the ball rolling." She slid her cell phone out of the breast pocket of her denim shirt. "I'll send his office a text now to see if he can see us."

"But Angela. What if he isn't actually gone for good? What if he comes back?"

Angela didn't look up from the screen. "Then you get a court order to get him the hell out. Don't take him back this time. Just don't do it."

"I know but…"

"Yup. He says he's got an opening at 9:30." She put the phone away. "I'll come down and get you at 8:00 and we'll go for coffee first."

Lisa tried to say she couldn't go. She really wanted to say no, she wasn't ready to see a lawyer. She glanced out the window to where the lake lay as grey and still as steel just beyond the rooftops.

"Well…" she said. "I guess it won't hurt to just see what he says. I'll…I'll see you tomorrow."

⬏

When the cold sun touched her face next morning she rolled out of bed, ran to the bathroom, and retched. Oh no, she thought. I'm sick. I can't go anywhere today. Crawling back to her empty bed she clutched the blankets up to her chin. But five minutes later she had to crawl out again to answer the door.

"I thought you'd be ready by now." Angela breezed in. "C'mon, honey. We gotta get going."

"I'm sick today, Angela. I really should stay…"

"Don't be silly. It's just nerves. You get dressed while I make the coffee." A minute later Lisa heard water running.

"Oh, and what about wearing your blue dress," came the voice from her kitchen. "Most of your other clothes make you look a bit mousy."

The navy blue wool dress did fit her well. She didn't wear it often because it seemed a bit fancy. Its slim lines and bright white trim at the collar and cuffs portrayed an image she felt she couldn't live up to. She smoothed the blue wool over bony hips, catching the small flash in the mirror of the diamond on her hand.

"Looks great. I thought it would," said Angela from the doorway. "Come have coffee then we gotta get going."

She went to the kitchen and sat down with a cup of coffee. "Angela," she said, "I don't think I can do this."

"Of course you can, Honey. And it's long overdue."

They walked together down morning streets with the town already bustling.

They found the lawyer's tiny office upstairs from the candy shop. Angela introduced her to the lawyer then turned to her and said, "I can't stay, Lisa. I have to get to work but I expect you to get this sorted out." She flashed a huge smile to the lawyer. "Thanks for doing this for me, Mike. I appreciate it. And so does Lisa."

"But Angela…?" Lisa stammered as the door swung closed behind her friend. She wanted to run back down the stairs and out into the crisp sunlight.

"Please, sit down Mrs. Campbell. We'll get started." Mike closed the door and cut off the sound of Angela's footsteps on the stairs.

Lisa stared at him and swallowed hard. She owed it to Angela to stay and see this through. After all, her friend had paid her rent this morning out of her own cookie jar money.

Mike was a kind, fussy little man who spoke in a quick, soft voice looking down at his desk the whole time. By the time she left his office she could remember almost nothing of what they talked about except the one thing that sang in her mind: "You are entitled to support payments and to half of all his assets. If he won't pay, then the government has the power to enforce those payments. Don't you worry, Mrs. Campbell. You will be looked after."

How reassuring those words were. She assumed, without Patrick, she couldn't survive on her wages alone. Now she knew she wouldn't have to.

She looked up toward the mountains as she trudged up Main Street. They were crowned in mists that swirled across the pine covered slopes. They looked so peaceful and soft the sight brought the hint of a smile to her lips.

"How do you feel about the idea of divorce?" Mike had asked.

"It terrifies me, quite honestly. It's so final. It's like the death of something."

"Well it is that," he said. "It's the death of a marriage. Some people grieve the end of a marriage. But think of it this way. What is your immediate reaction if I told you that Patrick would come home tonight and your life would resume as normal?"

Lisa felt an overwhelming sense of suffocation so dense she gasped. "Oh dear," she stuttered.

"I thought so. Now try to imagine what your immediate reaction would be if I told you that you never have to see him again and that you will be taken care of financially at the same level as before?"

"Really? Is that possible?" She could breathe again. The air flooded her lungs in a wave of relief.

"Yes, really. And there's your answer, Mrs. Campbell. Or should I say, Lisa. Now, let's get to work."

⁂

Over the next few weeks she saw Mike several more times to sign papers; she went in to work her shifts at the Copper Kettle; she cleaned and rearranged the apartment, packing up Patrick's things in boxes and storing them in the back of the closet. At first it felt like a dangerous game because she knew what he would do if he came home and found she had moved his things. Still, as each day flowed into the next with no word from her husband, she began to enjoy the decluttering. Each day each object she removed created a little more spaciousness and light in the apartment that had never been there before.

Angela came down for tea one afternoon and commented on the way the place looked. "I did the same thing when my husband left. Except I threw all his stuff out on the front lawn and set it on fire."

"You didn't!"

"Yeah. I did. Good riddance I say."

"Didn't he ever come back and want his things?"

"No. He called me from Reno when the divorce papers finally found him. He screamed at me over the phone and I just hung up on him. Never heard from him again."

"Don't you ever miss him? I kind of miss Patrick. At least I think I do."

"Oh, sure. You miss them for a while but that's just habit more than anything. It's like missing an old pair of slippers that were so worn out you tossed 'em in the garbage. You miss how comfortable they used to be even though they hadn't been that way for a long time."

"Yes, I guess that's what I miss. It's the comfort of having someone in your life." But in truth she knew she didn't even want him to come back.

At the end of two weeks she was able to pay Angela back from her pay check and she was surprised to find she still had money left over. When Patrick had taken her pay checks each time he said they barely covered the rent. His pay went into a savings account for their future. At least that's what he said.

On payday she left the Copper Kettle with a fellow worker and they went together to the bank. Just outside the bank there were a group of young people in long, black coats with nose rings and greasy hair asking everyone for spare change. The woman she was with clutched her handbag closer under her arm.

"They're always around on pay day. They know when we've got money," she hissed. "Don't worry about them. They manage just fine without our 'spare' change. Just say no."

But one of them touched Lisa's arm. "Spare change, Miss? Just for a cup of coffee?"

"Yes, yes, of course," she said as she tried to back away from the young man's grip to rummage in her purse. Her co-worker looked at her in disgust, shook her head and walked away. Lisa gave the grubby hand a dollar then turned her body to slide past him.

She realized at once what she had done; given in again. But honestly he did look hungry. They all did. She knew about that. She had been eating nothing but macaroni and bread all week so as not to have to ask Angela for any more money.

But not tonight! After leaving the bank she walked up to the By-Way market and picked up a few groceries. The fresh fish counter had always been off limits before. Patrick hated fish. He only liked meat: steak, chops, meatloaf and roasts. The salmon fillets looked so light and inviting she decided to splurge. Then she added another illicit treat: fresh mushrooms. After paying for the groceries the rest of the precious bills were tucked back into the pay envelope and hidden in the bottom of her purse.

She felt bravely guilty about the expense and yet somehow the weight of the grocery bags gave her the strange sensation that they were all that anchored her to the ground. If she wished, she could sail quietly up to her third floor window with ease. Instead she took the stairs, ignoring Mrs. Baker's half open door.

While the mushrooms sizzled in butter she chilled a bottle of wine she took from its hiding place in the back of the cupboard behind the oatmeal. It had been her Christmas gift from her boss last year and luckily Patrick had never found it.

She made herself a small salad. It felt strange to be doing these things for herself. It was like something out of a Women's magazine: "Dining for One". With Patrick it was steak and onions, hash browns and beer and too often the steak was not cooked to his liking so he would stomp off to the hotel for a hamburger and beer.

Just as she dropped the salmon fillet into the hot frying pan the buzzer rang at the apartment door. Without security in the building it could be anyone. She was tempted to ignore it as she usually did but after the second long buzz she went to the door. Irritated by the interruption she opened the door a little more forcefully than she had intended.

The man standing in the hallway was suave and stylish in a chestnut suit, pale brown shirt and bright white tie. He held a clipboard filled with colourful brochures in one tanned hand.

"Good evening, Ma'am," he said with a Cheshire cat smile. "I'm with Miracle Cable Systems and we're installing high speed fibre optics in your building and we'd like to include you. May I have a few minutes of your time?"

"Well…it's not really a good time," she said as she looked back over her shoulder in the direction of the kitchen.

The man nodded sympathetically. "Of course, but you see we're only coming through doing these installations once so anybody who doesn't sign up will have to pay a lot more if they decide to have it installed in the future. Now I'm just going to show you some price comparisons." He removed one of the glossy brochures from his clipboard and began to open it. "What's your internet speed now?"

"I…I don't know really. I'm sorry."

"No problem. I can check that easily enough. If I can come in for a moment I can just take a quick look at your computer system and…" He took a step forward. Lisa waited for the familiar wave of fear but instead an unfamiliar sensation of anger began to build behind her eyes.

"Excuse me, but I'm in the middle of cooking dinner." She gestured vaguely toward the kitchen and bit her lip at her own rudeness but it was her first meal with her own money and it was burning, she knew it.

"You're probably only running a download speed of 940

megabytes per second. Most people in this building are. How would you like to increase your download speed up to 1500 mbps with no more than a small increase in your monthly costs?" The man hadn't even acknowledged what she said.

"You don't understand. I'm not interested. I hardly use the computer anyway."

"Well, perhaps your husband would have a moment to speak to me?" His smile was brittle now and barely covered his teeth.

She stared at him. "My husband's not…he doesn't…" She paused. It was none of this man's business. "I don't have a husband," she said firmly.

"Oh. I'm sorry." He smirked. "Let me just leave my card then and if you change your mind…"

Sorry? What on earth was he sorry about? That she didn't have a husband or that he didn't make the sale?

"No, thank you," Lisa said firmly and closed the door in the man's face.

She latched the door and sprinted for the kitchen. She rescued the salmon just beginning to brown. 'Thank goodness', she thought. She slid it onto a warmed plate, piled the mushrooms on top and added the salad. Half way to the table with the plate in her hand she stopped. She glanced at the closed apartment door.

She had said "No"! She had stood up for herself. It might be a small thing to someone else but to Lisa it felt like a victory. A tiny victory but it meant that maybe, just maybe, she could do this.

Lisa Campbell sat down to her first meal as a single woman.

It wasn't going to be impossible after all.

Chapter 4
Making Magic
(December)

The farm was ten minutes south of town, down a packed dirt road which, at this time of year, became snow-covered ruts. The tires on Nicole's Jeep cut solidly into the icy crust and she had no trouble pulling into the farm yard. Her mother-in-law's stucco farmhouse with a bright blue roof stood out against the distant stand of olive green pines Jean's husband had planted decades ago as a wind break. The green of the pines was diluted now by the icing sugar dusting of snow.

The front door banged shut and Jean came down the steps, looking regal as always. Jean stood 5'6" and was still strong and fit; a physique that stood her in good stead now that she was a widow trying to keep up with farm work on her own. Her silver hair was the only real clue to her age.

Still, it was obvious that Jean was not managing to keep on top of things. The paint on the windows and doors of the house was shabbier than Nicole had ever seen it. Martin had touched up the bright white trim every year while he was still alive. One side of the chicken coop door was drooping and looked like it had been secured with wire ties. The tractor was sitting out in the snow.

But Jean was proud and determined to keep the farm so there wasn't much anyone could say.

"Hey Jean," Nicole called, getting out of the Jeep. "How are you?"

"Doing fine, Nicole. How are you?"

"Good. I made shortbread cookies to share. I assume you made your famous mincemeat tarts?"

"I did indeed," replied Jean, holding up a plastic wrapped dish.

The women secured the tart and cookie tins in the trunk then drove into town. Harry's gas station was busy with several cars lined up at the pumps but Harry took a moment to wave as they passed.

"Harry's a good man you know, Jean. He's helped us out a lot over the years," Nicole said.

Her mother-in-law turned in the passenger seat to glare fully at Nicole. "I'm not interested, Nicole. I'm fine." Jean's silver hair was tied up in a braid that draped down her back. Her strong features were still attractive and her age didn't show in her face yet. Nicole knew that Harry had been interested in Jean for years; long before Martin died if the truth were known.

She sighed. "I know, Jean. I know. I'm just saying."

She parked outside the bakery and they walked over to City Hall. The other volunteers were standing in the snow drinking coffee. Thermoses melted circles in the snow at their feet. They greeted friends and neighbours and chatted for a few minutes until the Volunteer Fire Department ladder truck pulled up.

Matt jumped out of the cab of the truck and gave his mother a hug. He kissed Nicole and greeted the others gathered on the curb. His friend, Kenny, stepped down from the driver's side of the fire truck. They were both in their fire department uniforms, even though there was no fire. It was policy that they could not be out in the truck in civvies.

"Okay guys," Matt said. "Let's get to work."

Nicole had always looked forward to the tradition of turning the town into a Christmas fairy land. She felt it was one of the great perks of small town life. The transformation in one afternoon was magical.

She watched as her husband maneuvered the ladder truck into position to attach light strings to the tops of each of the trees that lined Main St. The guys on the truck grabbed the lights and wound them down to the point where the people on the ground could finish winding to the bottom branches. As the truck moved up the street, passersby stopped to watch the work and little kids swarmed the truck.

Nicole smiled as she watched Matt. He was always patient with the kids and would describe how things on the shiny red truck worked. Kenny grumbled and refused to turn on the siren no matter how many times a little voice begged.

She felt a swell of pride watching her husband work.

When both sides of the street were done, Matt and Kenny strung the final set of lights with the red star in the middle across the main entrance off the highway. Then they took the truck back to the station. The rest of the group gathered for a break at the picnic table in the park, brushing snow from the benches and putting down blankets to sit on.

Jean and Nicole brought out the baked treats from Nicole's trunk and passed them around. They all shared coffee and hot chocolate that anyone had left in their thermoses plus the cookies and tarts and other goodies people brought. Conversation swirled around the familiar topics and what people were doing for Christmas.

"Hey there they are," someone called.

Kenny and Matt were trudging back down the street toward them carrying the last box that had been stored at the fire hall. They dropped the box on the ground.

"So you didn't save us any of my own Mom's famous tarts?" cried Matt. "What gives you guys?"

Jean smiled. She opened the small backpack she had been carrying and handed a cookie tin to her son.

"I've never let you go hungry in your life, son. I'm not about to start now."

Matt opened the tin and popped a tart in his mouth whole. He gave her a hug, leaving pastry crumbs on the shoulder of her jacket. He grabbed another tart and handed the tin to Kenny. Then he sat down beside Nicole.

"Hey Kenny," Nicole said. "Lynn didn't come down to join the fun today. Is she okay?' She poured a lukewarm hot chocolate for him from the big orange plastic thermos.

"Nah." He took the cup with one big hand and scrubbed the other through his red-blond mat of hair. "She's got one of her migraines again. She gets so sick with 'em she can't get out of bed."

"I'm sorry to hear that. I've asked a friend of mine to stop in and see her. She might be able to help. Should I take her some goodies to make up for missing today?"

"She'd like that," said Kenny.

Nicole poured the dregs of the hot chocolate into a cup and handed it to Matt. "Sorry Matt," she said. "That's all we have left." She rested her hand on his arm. "I could get you some coffee from the Copper Kettle?"

"This is fine, Honey." He drank half the drink and put the cup down. She knew he would forget where he put it so she grabbed the cup and placed it carefully behind the orange thermos jug.

The rest of the volunteers opened the box the men had brought and fanned out to string large silver snowflakes onto every lamppost on both sides of the street all the way back to

City Hall. The final touch was to hang a Christmas wreath on the hook above the war memorial.

Finally they were able to stand back to admire the magic they had created. The afternoon was darkening enough to see the lights strung in elegant swirls around all the neatly spaced trees planted in sidewalk insets along Main Street. The effect was a fairy palace lit with candles for a ball. The lights twinkled behind the drifting snowflakes and the town took on the magic of the Christmas season in one afternoon. The mountains stood in brooding contrast in the background, still showing dark beneath their light coats of snow. By Christmas they would be as perfectly white as a child's smile.

Finally the volunteers said goodbye and drifted away.

"I always thought this would be the perfect time to break out the song books and sing Christmas carols," Jean said to Nicole as they helped clear up the used cups and napkins. "I suggested it several times at town council meetings but everyone thought that would be 'corny'."

"I don't think so," Nicole said. "I think that would be nice….Whoaaaa!" she yelped. Matt had come up behind her and grabbed her around the waist.

"Gotcha," Matt grinned and kissed Nicole on the cheek then brushed snow from her hair. "Just going for a drink with the guys. I'll see you later at home." Nicole scowled at him but he had turned away.

Jean and Nicole decided to walk over to the Copper Kettle restaurant for supper.

"That feels good," Nicole sighed as she dropped into a chair. "My feet are so sore." Her feet were cold so she surreptitiously slipped off her boots and rested her feet on top of them to get warm air circulating.

"I know what you mean. I'm not used to being on my feet

in my good boots so long," Jean grimaced as she took a chair beside her daughter-in-law.

"So how's work these days?" she asked.

Nicole sipped her tea before answering. "It's fine," she sighed. "I'm just really tired lately. It must be the winter blues. Whew."

Jean put her hand over Nicole's. "Darling girl, are you sure? You do look quite pale, not meaning to be rude or anything. Is there anything I can help you with?"

"Thanks, Jean. I'm sure I'll be all right. I just need some rest."

"All right. If you're sure." She picked up her menu. "So what should we have then?" Jean asked. "My treat."

"I'm really not very hungry," Nicole said. "I'm actually a bit nauseated."

Jean glanced at Nicole who shrugged and grinned back.

"Well I'm famished," sighed Jean. "I'm going to eat enough tonight so I don't have to cook for myself again for a week. I hate cooking for one anyway." There was a note of sadness in her voice.

Nicole was staring at her hands and twisting her wedding ring around on her finger so she didn't pick up on the tone.

"So do I," she replied glumly. She looked up at her mother-in-law and Jean was surprised to see tears shimmering just at the point of spilling.

"Nicole, what's wrong?"

"Matt just never seems to be home anymore. I didn't want to mention it. It's just…I'm starting to get worried."

"About what?"

"I've been really grouchy lately. I try not to be but it just happens. And Matt has been spending more and more time away from home. I don't know what to do." The tears rolled over her cheeks.

"Oh Nicole, I'm so sorry. Where on earth does he go then?"

"He spends most of his time out with those two idiots he calls his friends. Mostly at the bar, I guess. I eat alone more nights than I don't. He was away all afternoon yesterday, as a matter of fact."

"I know. He was up at the farm helping me put up the Christmas lights and the tree. Didn't you know he was going to be doing that?"

"No," she wiped her eyes with a napkin. "I didn't. He never tells me these things. Back in September he planned an entire weekend away on a hunting trip and didn't even tell me. A whole weekend! I had to find out from one of the other guys' wives. The whole town knew before I did that my husband was going away for a weekend without me."

"But, Nicole, he didn't end up going without you, did he? Wasn't that the camping trip you all went on together? You and the three men?"

Nicole sniffed. "Yes, I know. But I kind of had to railroad them into that." She smiled a bit sheepishly.

Jean laughed. "I heard."

"What can I bring you ladies?" The waitress stood by the table with no pad or pencil in hand. Her greying hair was cut in a rather cute pixie cut that somehow didn't quite suit her lined face but she was friendly and patient as she took their orders. Nicole had seen her in the café many times and sometimes on the street but she never was able to remember the woman's name. She glanced at the name tag on the woman's uniform. Lisa it said in a nice script font.

The waitress listened and nodded then walked away without writing anything down or even repeating it back to them.

"I'll be very surprised if we actually get what we ordered," Nicole whispered, frowning.

Jean gave her a brief smile. "Nicole," she said. "People aren't perfect and marriage isn't perfect. It takes work and it takes compromise."

"I know that but..."

Jean put her work roughened hand over Nicole's. It felt warm and comforting.

"As I said it's never perfect but having someone warm and loving to lean on is worth more than gold. You think that's not enough. Maybe not, but add the knowledge that there's someone who cares about you, who'll be there for you in bad times, who'll hold you when you cry, someone who cares more about you than anyone else on the planet. You can forgive an awful lot of foolish behaviour in exchange for that. Believe me. I'm alone out there on our farm every day since Martin died and every day I think about him and miss him."

"Oh Jean. I didn't mean to bring up sad memories."

"You didn't, dear. It's fine but you know, my marriage wasn't ideal either. I hate to admit it but Martin was a bit boring. Don't ever tell Matt I said that about his Dad, but he never wanted to do anything. All our lives I kept hoping we would travel when we retired. That we would do something adventurous, something fun. Martin never wanted to leave Cougar Lake, not even for short trips. And now he's gone and I'm too old."

"You are not too old!" Nicole answered. "You've got lots of life left. You can't give up on life."

"And neither can you. Or give up on your marriage either." She pointed her teaspoon at Nicole. "You and Matt have only been married a few months. You've got to give him a chance to get used to the idea of being a husband."

"I know, Jean. I know."

Their meals arrived at that moment. To their surprise, their orders were faithfully presented and very good.

"You know," Nicole veered off the subject as she poked at her salad. "Matt and I do worry about you out there alone on the farm."

"Oh, I'm all right mostly," Jean said. "At least during the day. The nights are hard. I miss him most at night. Nighttime makes you vulnerable to memories. It feels like he's there sometimes."

"But what are you going to do when January blizzards come in and the roads are blocked?" Nicole asked.

"I'll manage the same way we always did. Have enough supplies to last until the guys can get out with the plow."

"Okay but what about next summer," Nicole asked. "What about planting and harvesting? You're surely not planning on trying to put in crops on your own?"

"I can hire someone to do the heavy work and Matt says he'll help."

Nicole dropped her fork onto her salad plate with a rattle. "See? That's exactly what I'm talking about. He says these things and commits himself without once asking me or talking to me about it. And while he's helping everyone else the things around our place sit and fall apart. That's so typical!"

There was silence at the table. Jean stared at her daughter-in-law.

"Oh Jean," Nicole cried, realizing what she'd said. "I didn't mean it that way. Really I didn't. Of course we'll help you. We both will. I didn't mean we wouldn't or that he shouldn't or…"

"It's alright," Jean said quietly. "I understand what you meant. You're right to be frustrated with him. But the problem, as I see it, is one of communication between the two of you. It's not just a problem of him being wrong and you being right, you know."

"I know. I'm sorry." Nicole's heart shaped face was drawn and tense.

"It's almost Christmas," Jean said with a brighter tone. "Families should be making magic together, not fussing. We've just had a great day. Why don't you and Matt come back to my place? We'll light a fire and have a glass of wine and a game of Yahtzee. The tree is even up, not decorated, but up?"

Nicole shook her head. "I'd better head home. Matt's probably home by now. But thanks, Jean. Another time. But listen, why don't you take the Jeep. I can easily walk from here." Nicole passed her the jeep keys. "We can pick it up from you tomorrow."

Nicole scrounged in her purse for the money to pay for her salad but her mother-in-law stopped her.

"My treat."

"Thanks Jean," Nicole said. Jean stood and hugged her in a firm, warm embrace.

"I'll see you soon, dear."

Out on the street the snow had stopped and the coloured strings of lights glistened like tiny rainbows along the street. The shops were shut now but there was still light streaming from the other coffee shop and several of the bars. Main Street was unusually quiet under a fresh blanket of sound proofing. Nicole had always loved the hush of a new snowfall. Normal ambient sound disappeared into the softness. She hoped Christmas would be like this.

More importantly she hoped she could feel the joy she thought should be part of this first Christmas as Matt's wife and the joy she should be feeling about the baby. So far it had proved impossible for her to open her mouth and tell anyone about the baby. Her friend Megan had guessed of, course, but Nicole refused to confirm or deny it. She suspected Jean might be wondering too.

She should be happy, shouldn't she? A baby was a kind of

magic. Something was being created that hadn't existed before. A little human being was forming inside her. She and Matt would do what almost every married couple who ever lived had done, start a family. Isn't that what she wanted? It's not like she was planning on making a career out of her job. She could give that up tomorrow. It was her dreams she was having trouble giving up. Like the scholarship she had been awarded from the Canadian Forest Service to get her degree as a Park Ranger. That wasn't going to be possible now.

So many pathways that had been open to her would be blocked, so many doors would close. Would she regret this?

Because of the snow she didn't hear the car pull up until it stopped beside her. A single headlight shone onto the marshmallow street, the other headlight had yet to be fixed.

"Hey Babe. I've been looking all over for you. Where ya bin?"

"I had supper with your Mom." Nicole climbed into the car and brushed the snow from her coat before turning to her husband.

"How come you didn't tell me you were going to meet Mom for supper? I didn't know where you were," Matt said.

"Well I didn't know where you were yesterday afternoon either," she said.

"So…does that mean we're even?" His eyes shone hopefully in the subdued light inside the car. Red and green and gold colour flashed across the hood of the Chevy as he pulled away from the curb. His wedding ring caught the colours too as he swung his hand across the top of the steering wheel to bring the car into the driving lane.

"I guess," she said. She sat quietly watching the lake shimmering in the snowy light until they were almost home.

"Matt?"

"Hmmm?"

"I know we've talked about this before but I just wondered: do you want kids? I mean really?"

"Of course I do. You know I do."

"If we had a kid things would have to be a lot different. You would have to be home to help. You couldn't go off with the boys after work every day and come home whenever you felt like it. I would have to know I could count on you to be there, you know."

"Babe, I absolutely would. I would be the best father in the world. I promise. I do want a bunch of little rug rats running around and I know my Mom would just bust with joy. Maybe we could try, whenever you feel ready. We could try. What d'ya think."

Nicole stared out the windshield at the single beam of light shining as Matt pulled into the yard in front of their trailer.

"I think we already did," she said in a whisper.

Matt slammed on the brake. The car skidded and spat snow. He sat still for a moment, gripping the steering wheel. Slowly he turned to face her. The look of wonder on his face was something she had never seen before.

"No way!" he said. "For real?"

Nicole nodded.

Matt reached for his wife and gathered her into his arms and hugged her so tightly she had trouble catching her breath.

"Oh Honey! This is the most wonderful, magical, totally awesome Christmas present I've ever had."

He pulled back and looked into her eyes. "I promise, promise, promise, Honey. I will be the best Daddy you've ever seen. I will take such good care of you and the ..."

"Matt! The car!"

"Shit!" He grabbed the wheel, pressed the brake again and

shoved the gear shift into park. "Sorry, sorry, I took my foot off the brake for a second there. Sorry Honey."

"So this is how you're going to take care of me and the baby?"

"No Geez. No."

"It's okay Matt. I'm teasing. I know you would never let anything happen to us." Us, she thought. It isn't just me now. It's us.

"I wouldn't. I swear. Oh Babe. I am just so happy I can't even spit. Let's go in and celebrate. I'll make you a big mug of hot chocolate and take you to bed." He stopped. "That is okay still, isn't it?"

"Yeah," Nicole smiled. "It's okay."

Chapter 5
The Quiet Months of Winter
(January)

In the New Year snow settled down over the town, the lake, and the surrounding hills. It hissed gently as it fell into the black water. Gradually ice fanned out from the lake shore like Chinese lace.

By late January the lake froze solidly enough for skaters to venture out onto the ice. The guys from the fire department were often found down at the lake skimming along with wide shovels in front of them. They cleared meandering pathways of ice for the skaters. The swish and crunch of skate blades as they slid across the rough surface echoed in the crisp air. In some places the ice was clear enough to see down into a magic world of ice bubbles.

Young people walked down the quiet lanes to the lake in the evenings. They wore warm woolen gloves and colourful knitted caps. Their skates, slung over their shoulders, glistened in the yellow cones of streetlights.

In the afternoons it would be the kids from the high school who grabbed the bent and battered shovels that always sat propped up in a snow bank all winter long. The kids would clear enough ice for a game of hockey. Later they tossed the shovels up onto the bank and piled into cars and pickups to head to someone's house for pizza and beer.

The snow fell straight and steady, day after day, from a

windless sky in a soft infusion of white. Silent pillows closed off one house from another and fires burned in fireplaces, flickering orange and amber against curtained windows. Voices were hushed in the living rooms. Snow piled up on roofs and made the rafters groan with the weight.

The foothills to the west dreamed under their white blankets. Cars along the highway whooshed past with a whistle of slush beneath their tires. Carl from the repair shop got out his Ford F150 with the blade on the front and clattered up and down Main Street leaving cut lines of snow behind any car foolish enough to be parked there on an early Saturday morning in January.

On a grey Monday morning a face was watching through a slit in the blinds of a small house on the last street at the edge of town. It was only six blocks from Main Street but beyond was farm land. The shabby siding and drooping eaves made the house look sad. No light shone through the grimy windows even though the day was heavily overcast. All the blinds were down.

Lynn lifted the blinds just enough to peer out, watching for her expected visitor. She saw Matt and Nicole drive by in Matt's old rattle trap Chevy. Automatically she lifted her hand to wave to them but, of course, she realized, they couldn't see her.

Just then a shiny blue Ford Ranger came to a stop in the deep snow in front of the house. A tall, slim woman with raven hair and cowhide boots emerge from the truck and tromped up the un-cleared walk to her door. The bell rang; a faint chime sounded inside the house, then silence. She dropped the blinds, scrubbed a hand through her hair, and opened the door.

"I'm Rachel," the woman said. "Rachel Eaglesclaw."

"Hi," Lynn replied softly and she opened the door wider.

The woman stepped inside and immediately Lynn saw her face register distaste. Lynn cringed. Even though she lived here she could still smell the musty odor of the old house overlaid with fried bacon and toast. It made her claustrophobic for a moment and she knew that was what her guest was reacting to. It was humiliating.

"Please, come in," she said hurriedly. "I thought we could talk in the kitchen." At least in the kitchen there was a window she could open. She led the way into the tiny kitchen with one small window with the blinds down and curtains drawn. She lifted the blinds just enough to slide the window open a crack, wincing at the pain in her head.

"Please sit down" Lynn gestured to two vinyl kitchen chairs beside a round wooden table.

Rachel stayed standing. "I'll need a kettle to make the tea." She set her bag on the table and began taking out wild herbs to make into a tea.

Lynn filled the kettle with water and plugged it in then sat down.

"Tell me about the headaches."

As she began to describe her symptoms she watched this rather intimidating woman setting up little bags of dried herbs, a small spoon, a darkly stained earthen ware bowl and a tiny metal strainer. What had she been thinking letting this stranger into her house? Nicole said this lady worked with her at the senior's home but she hadn't expected someone like this. She had expected someone older. More soft and kind like a nurse. Although, she had to admit, Nicole hadn't said she was a nurse. Only that she was knowledgeable about the native healing arts. She watched Rachel's long black braid swing gracefully as she worked.

"Does it hurt right now?"

"Yes," Lynn said. "That's why all the blinds are down. I can't stand the light. I'm really grateful to you for coming over. Nicole said you don't live here in town?"

"I live on the reserve. West up the Bow River Valley."

"That's a long way to come."

"I don't mind the drive," Rachel said. "How long have you been having these migraines?"

Lynn looked up and found Rachel watching her with piercing charcoal eyes.

"Years now really," she said. "I don't even remember when they started but some days I can't even get out of bed."

She didn't mention the overwhelming tired sadness that kept her in bed even on days without the headaches. She didn't say that the headaches seemed joined to the sense of aimlessness in her life. She didn't know this woman.

Nicole had said no one knew Rachel very well. Apparently she kept pretty much to herself. In fact, Nicole said when she had told her, during a rare shared coffee break, about Lynn's chronic, debilitating migraine headaches Rachel had said, "I could fix those." Then had looked as though she instantly regretted it.

"So you work with Nicole at the senior's home?"

"No. She's a duty nurse. I work downstairs in administration."

"You're not a nurse?" Lynn could hear the tremble in her own voice. "I mean, not that you would need to be of course."

"No, I'm not." Rachel's hands stopped moving and her dark eyes were challenging.

Lynn looked down at the table. "Do you do this as a part time job?" Nicole hadn't said anything about paying Rachel but now she worried that she might have misunderstood.

"No," Rachel said cryptically.

"Oh." What could she say to that? "What are these herbs?" she asked to change the subject.

"Mint leaf, willow bark, red raspberry leaf, chamomile blossom, rosemary, yarrow and dandelion root." She pointed at each little bag as she spoke.

"How did you learn so much about these things?"

Rachel sighed and sat down at the kitchen table. Swung her ebony hair across one shoulder but she didn't answer. Lynn suddenly felt foolish even asking the question. Obviously it would be an ancient art inherited at her mother's or grandmother's knee.

Finally Rachel spoke without looking up, "I'm a Certified Herbalist. I studied at Pacific Rim College on Vancouver Island."

Lynn was stunned. She sat back in the wobbly kitchen chair. Nicole hadn't said anything about that. Did she even know this? It was one thing not to know a lot about a co-worker who worked in an entirely different area of the home than she did but that something so fundamental was not common knowledge at the home was surprising. It was not a huge staff. Perhaps Rachel deliberately kept this skill a secret although Lynn couldn't imagine why.

"Why on earth are you working in the office if you have that kind of training?"

"Because it's my job." Rachel said sharply. Her dark eyes seemed to have no pupils. "Now watch how I pour this. You don't just slop the boiled water onto the herbs, you gently slide the water underneath them then, as it steeps, the herbs gradually absorb the water and sink."

"Thank you, Rachel. Really. I so appreciate you taking the time to do this. I'm pretty much at my wits end."

"You're welcome." Rachel's dark eyes softened. "Bothers me

to see someone suffer when the natural ways can help so much. Did you try any herbal remedies?"

"I tried peppermint tea. Also tried acupuncture plus lots of pain meds, prescription and over the counter. Nothing helps or at least not for long."

"Don't touch that stuff. Doctors are rewarded by the big pharmaceutical companies to peddle their drugs. These will not harm you. They work with your body; not against it. These herbs have been used by women for centuries. Where's your husband?"

Lynn was silent for a moment, not quite following the leap of logic. "He's at work. He works up at the Lafarge plant near Exshaw."

"I live just outside Exshaw. My family used to fish on Lac Des Arcs." She paused to gently swirl the water in the tea bowl. "Did you know Exshaw Mountain is known locally as Cougar Mountain? Seems the mountain and the town are connected."

Lynn tried to follow this thread then Rachel put a small, handless ceramic cup in front of her and poured the tea through a strainer. It smelled of mint but there was also a musty, earthy smell she couldn't identify.

"Can I put some honey in it?" She was almost afraid to ask in case it was an insult to the tea.

"Raw honey only. You got any?"

"Yes." Lynn got up to get the honey. "Are you having some?"

"Don't need it."

"Of course." She stirred the honey in and took a sip. It wasn't quite as awful as she had feared, but close.

"So that must be a long commute for you. I know it's almost an hour up Highway 40 for my husband, Kenny, to get to work."

"It's the same for me coming this way," Rachel said.

Lynn thought better of smiling at this.

"Have you thought of moving to Cougar Lake?"

Rachel's dark eyes flashed. There's a temper under there, thought Lynn. She didn't know what she had said that was wrong.

"Why should I move to a squalid little town like this?"

"Squalid?" Once again Lynn felt she was being challenged. "You think Cougar Lake is squalid?"

Rachel got up and began to pace around the small kitchen. "You've got a population of maybe 1,000 people living here? You're not mountain people but the mountains block you to the west. You're not prairie people but the prairie creeps up on you from the east. You're not farmers or ranchers or hunters. You have none of the benefits of the city. Not cultural, economic, educational. You don't even have a real hospital. If someone's really injured you have to make the run to Calgary. It's a nowhere place with no purpose. I should be asking you why you stay here. Surely you could get out of here and do something with your life?"

Lynn's face felt like she had just opened a hot oven door. Her throat closed over the angry but wordless retort that tried to rise. She gripped the tea cup in her hands so tightly she thought it might shatter. A careful, controlled swallow of tea. A breath of silence and she felt a little more ready to respond. She felt like she had to defend the town and her life, which was strange because normally she felt smothered by both.

"I have to admit I struggle with that. Quite often really." She took a deep breath. "But I think I am doing something with my life," she said to Rachel's stiff back. "I have a good job at the mercantile store. It's only part time but I could move up if I wanted to." She thought for a minute digging for reasons why her life mattered. " I'm married to a man I love. I admit my house needs some work but my headaches have made it impossible to keep up with things."

"Uh huh," Rachel said, not looking at her.

"Also," Lynn said, surprising herself, "I live in a community where I know everyone and they know me and we support each another. I don't see that kind of caring in the city but I see it here every day."

"I'm not saying the city's all that much better," Rachel said. "There are other options besides just a small town or a big city. But there's no opportunities here."

"But," said Lynn. "My family's here. There's a past here in Cougar Lake. There's history going back generations. That should mean something, shouldn't it?" She couldn't believe she was saying these things.

Rachel let out an explosive breath. "History! There's no past. The history of this town goes back a few hundred years. Out there we have a deeper history and a connection with the land and the mountains going back thousands of years. Our blood runs through the rocks and the rivers. We've always been a part of that valley."

Lynn put her empty cup down with more force that necessary. The flowered sugar bowl rattled on the table. She really had not expected a conversation like this. "So why are you here then?"

Rachel was silent. She stood and refilled Lynn's cup then motioned for her to drink. The electric clock in the living room clicked louder and louder with each passing minute. Snow hissed softly against the window. Lynn had just opened her mouth to apologize when the other woman slowly turned and sat down at the table again.

"I'll try to answer that," she said. "But first…are you feeling better yet?"

Lynn realized with surprise that she was. The pain behind her eyes was easing and there had been no waves of nausea for the past ten minutes at least. "I am. Yes. Thank you."

"Good." She sat in stillness again for a few minutes. Lynn had never known anyone who could sit so absolutely still. Not a muscle moved. Not a twitch. Finally Rachel spoke.

"I don't like to talk about myself much," she said. "But you asked. The job at the senior's home was the only one I could get. At least without going all the way to Calgary. I might have to end up going there but I don't belong there. Don't belong here either, although it's better. I belong out there." She gestured to the west." Her earth-dark fingers smoothed small crumbs from the table.

"Look, Lynn, sorry. I didn't mean to get into this. Just meant to come over to give you the tea. I have to go." Rachel abruptly got up from the table, gathered her things and grabbed her coat from the back of the chair. "Brew the tea like I showed you. Four times a day. When you need more just ask Nicole to get some from me."

"I will. Thank you, Rachel. I really appreciate it."

Rachel's pickup truck tires spat slush as she pulled out onto the road. Lynn lifted the blinds enough to watch until the truck disappeared behind a soft veil of snowflakes.

"What on earth was that about?" she whispered against the glass. As the fog circle of her breath cleared she saw Kenny's truck pull in before the snow had filled the tire ruts.

He let the front door slam behind him. "Hey Lynn. I'm home."

"No kidding," she said. She turned away from the window.

"Who was here? And why does this place smell like a haystack?" He dropped his keys in the bowl by the door and dumped his jacket on the chair so recently vacated by her guest.

"What's for dinner?"

She stared at him. His vanilla skin was covered at the moment with cement dust. Scruffy red hair was similarly dusted. An open, innocent face shadowed with stubble. But vitality radiated from him and a love of life sparkled in his green eyes. She had known him since kindergarten. His family was tied to hers in so many ways. And they were deeply rooted in this small Alberta town nestled in the foothills of the Rocky Mountains. The connections were intimate and sweet even if they didn't go back thousands of years.

She took Rachel's tea again at bedtime then 3 times a day for the following two days. She had a day off on Friday and felt well enough to try to tackle at least cleaning up the living room and bathrooms. It was a start.

When Kenny walked in the door that night he glanced at the tidy room then at her. "Hey Babe. You've been busy. We expecting company?"

"No." She walked over to him and stood on tiptoe to kiss his dry, cracked lips. "I love you, Kenny," she said.

"Wow," he said. He caught her around the waist and wrapped his arms around her. "What did I do to deserve this?"

"Never mind," she smiled. "Let's go down to the Burger Barn for supper. I'm hungry."

He held her away from him. "You feeling up to that?"

"Sure. Let me just go brush my hair and put on a sweater."

Kenny raised an eyebrow. "I was actually planning on going skating down at the lake with the guys after dinner. The ice is perfect for shooting nets. I could just drop you back home before I go. Would you be okay with that?"

Lynn stopped. Images flashed through her mind of the men sizzling down black ice chasing a puck in the light of the fire they would no doubt have going on the shore. Then images of herself sitting in their little house watching Netflix alone.

"I have a better idea," she said. "I'll bring a thermos of tea and a blanket and sit by the fire while you guys skate. The fresh air will do me good."

Kenny's caterpillar eyebrows quirked up again in surprise. "Seriously?" Then he grabbed his keys. "You got it, Darlin'. Let's go."

Chapter 6
Heartbeat On The Wind

(February)

Rachel Eaglesclaw had always known that her life was tangled inextricably in the letters of her name. Her father's proud tradition was written there, uneasily at war with the Catholic schooling her mother clung to still.

And working at Cougar Lake Senior's Home three days a week was not where she belonged. It was a dead end job. This was not her life. She refused to allow this to be her life.

She shivered and grabbed a thick-ribbed sweater from the pile on the closet shelf. She pulled it on over her flannel shirt and tugged it down to her hips.

The wind wrapped itself around the house like a wolf. The house sat alone on a slope over-looking the valley where Highway #1 ran to the mountains. Out here in the open it shuddered and gave up its heat to the hungry wind. The cold crept in at every corner, fighting the small heat from the old furnace. The Band money was due to come this week; if it didn't the propane tank would stay empty.

The house was small. From where she sat she could easily watch out the kitchen window and front window at the same time. Her father's truck would come from the west. Down from where Powderface Ridge stood against the sunset sky. Beyond that the Rocky Mountains rose like the crest of a giant Stegosaur. Toward the darkening east lay Calgary. It sprawled like a sickness across the prairie. When the young men and women went there they usually didn't come back.

Rachel would take the pickup truck tomorrow. She would drive into Calgary. But she would come back.

"Hurry up!" she said. They had to get this done before her father came home. The kitchen shears flashed in the hands of her cousin. She stood above Rachel, scowling.

"You shouldn't do this, Rachel," Marie said. "Why don't you just pin it up? Look." She wrapped Rachel's hair around her thick hands and held it on top of her head. "There," she said.

Marie's own dull braids hung limply on her chest like thin whips. She began to lose her hair after the third baby. Rachel looked at her cousin's hair, then in the mirror at her own mane, thick and shining black. Marie was only a year older and it hurt to see her fade like an old photograph left out in the sun, and yet Rachel couldn't help taking an evil pleasure in knowing her cousin envied her.

"Just do it!" she snapped. She pushed Marie's hands away and let the hair fall. Marie began to cry but she took up the scissors and started to snip. The hair dropped softly to the floor. Rachel didn't watch. She refused to weep for what was gone.

"I don't know why you want to do this," Marie sniffed and wiped her nose with the back of her hand. She squinted; concentrating hard on keeping the scissors level. "I would never. And I would never go there to live either."

"They want to hire our people. They have quotas. But they don't want me to look like one, okay? Don't you understand?"

The wind howled around the house, sniffing at the doors and windows for escaping warmth. There were no headlights yet bouncing up the rutted trail in the slushy snow. Rachel's mother sat in the living room watching television. The blue light flickered across her face like a sad fire. It was all she did now since her son, Rachel's younger brother, had died. He had been her dream and her pride. Rachel knew that. And she needed to see her mother's eyes shine with pride again somehow.

But now she rocked back and forth, moaning, chanting, watching. That's all. She accepted the food her husband brought, cooked it for the three of them. And watched TV. Rachel was the one who cleaned the house, when it got cleaned.

Her father worked at the Exshaw plant like a lot of the men out here. He usually drove in to Calgary with the other men from the plant on the weekends and sometimes didn't come home for a couple of days but he always managed to bring home enough groceries to feed them. At least he took care of that and at least he was still here. Marie's father was just gone. So many of the men just took off without a word and their families never heard from them again. Plenty of the ones who stayed weren't much good either. Rachel's father was a good man. He was not a man to walk away. But his job was hard and he was not a young man.

Rachel was determined to be able to care for herself and her parents too. She would move them from this house and buy an acreage somewhere out near Bragg Creek. Their own land; their own home.

"But you're giving up," Marie cried, interrupting her thoughts. "You always said you wouldn't! You said we have all given up. But you said you never would."

Rage like black wings opened wide within her chest. "I'm not giving up! The hair...it means nothing. What have we got left that means anything? We can't live in the old way; the men can't hunt in the old way. The animals have run from men who crawl and kill like cowards. The animals have lost the land and so have we. But I can win at the white man's game!"

Marie's face was streaked with tears. Marie was soft. Rachel breathed deeply to still the rage to protect her cousin.

"Marie," she said more calmly. "Remember when Eagle Dancer used to tell of powwows when he was a boy? How the bands all met and had games and danced and feasted? They played each other's games. It didn't matter who made up the game. It mattered who won."

Marie worked silently; the hair almost cut now. Rachel looked down; suddenly frightened by the dark feathers of hair already piling up around her feet.

"Marie," Rachel was surprised that her voice still came out strong and hard. "Marie? Do you really think it's so wrong? The government will give them money to hire me. They will pay me for work I do. I can come back with pride. It's a time for a new beginning for me. Don't you see that?"

"No," she cried. She gave a final snip and stepped back, waving the scissors. "Once you've made money you won't come back. I know it! This that you give up… this was your heritage!" She held the last handful of inky strands and let them fall between her fingers.

Rachel seethed. She grabbed one of her cousin's braids and pulled hard. "Does this make you Nakoda? No! This," she says, thumping her chest above her heart with her other hand. "This makes you Nakoda!"

Still holding her braid, Rachel grabbed for the open scissors but Marie sensed her intent and whipped them away. Rachel caught only one open blade.

"What is there here for me, Marie?" Blood welled up in the palm of her hand. "Look at her!" Rachel pointed to the blue light in the living room. "Look at this!" Her hand sprayed tiny drops of blood around the cramped kitchen; speckling the linoleum. "What real choice is there?"

"What about my life?" Marie sobbed. "What is so terrible about a husband and babies? With Billy's pay and the Band distribution we do okay."

Her eyes were the startled black of a rabbit in a snare. Her whimpering made Rachel want to claw her eyes. But she also felt a swell of shame. Marie was the one producing sons. She was content to live here on the land of their fathers. She was still true Nakoda.

The words she had said to Lynn a few weeks ago came back to haunt her now. "Out there we have a deep history and a connection with the land and the mountains going back thousands of years. Our blood runs through the rocks and the rivers up there. We've always been a part of that valley."

She had meant it then. And she meant it now. It's just that the world didn't work that way anymore. That life had drifted away with the wind. Now she needed to make a place in the new way of things.

Frustration boiled in her blood. She grabbed at the scissors again and twisted them from Marie's hand. She threw them across the room. Her mother startled like a deer.

"Aieee, aieee," she moaned, then turned back to watching TV. Woven into the ever-present chatter of the television Rachel could hear intense voices demanding, always demanding, wanting and winning sums of money so huge they were incomprehensible.

"You," she screamed at Marie, "You produce babies to get more money from the Band distribution. It doesn't help, though, does it? Billy's got that money spent before you even get it, just like everybody else. You're no better than me. Don't pretend you are!"

"Rachel!" Marie cried. "Rachel!" Her voice faded in the dingy light as Rachel grabbed the keys to the pickup and slammed the door.

She loved Marie and she couldn't stand her. She was too soft, too kind. In so many ways she envied her cousin but she couldn't be like that. Refused to be like that. The roar of the engine drowned her thoughts. The pickup rattled across the snow rutted ground. She turned onto Highway 40, barely missing the beautiful old red Chev as it sped past. A familiar car. One she had often admired when she saw it in town. It was tenacious and stubbornly refused to give up. Just like her.

She turned onto the dirt road that dove straight and true across the valley to the lonely place near the shoulder of Loder Peak. It was only a stand of spindly spruce on a wide rocky ledge but it was a high and quiet place that she loved. It always helped her to see the moon in a midday sky; to feel the wind on an airless day. A place where memories of buffalo and dreams of glory still whispered in the wind. A place she needed to go to tonight.

A roll of clouds climbed the face of Loder Peak like a smoke dragon emerging in the twilight. Crows swirled in the last of the evening light. They graced the land with their shadows.

Her fingers tightly gripped the wheel; the dark of her skin pale, almost white at the knuckles. She was not proud of what she was doing but the war was lost long before her birth. She would lose ground but she had a dream. The Elders are not the only ones who dream.

The truck climbed steadily into the mountains on the north side of the valley. Eventually she stopped and turned the key off. The engine shuddered into silence. Her hand came away sticky from the wheel and she realized the cut from the scissor blade, although not deep, was still bleeding. She had nothing to wrap it with so she wiped the blood off on her jeans then slipped on a pair of gloves and clenched her fist tightly to stop the blood.

She stepped from the truck and heard, over the click of the cooling engine, the peaceful sounds of the night. She stood still to listen, to identify each rustle of grouse, whisper of pine and distant call of owl. The scents of snow and wet sage rose from the valley. On the wind she could taste the tang of the pines and spruce. It was a strange mix here in this place where the worlds of the prairie and mountain met.

The snow was cold beneath her worn boots. She had a thick sweater under her jacket; the chill of the mountain didn't bother her as she walked up the faint game trail to the ledge.

Cars smoked along the highway in the distance; long golden eyes blazing in the deepening twilight. It seemed darker down there than where she stood. She could still see the last of the sun snared, for a moment, in Devils Gap.

The Exshaw plant was sending up a column of white smoke. It caught the light and glowed like fresh snow under the winter moon. She couldn't understand how anything that looked so pure and beautifully white could be so filthy it sickened the earth. But she knew the dust clung to everything for miles around: it clung, it smothered, it killed.

Rachel focused her thoughts on tomorrow. The man said the interview would be a formality.

"He said it was because I have the skills they need but I know that's only part of it. What he didn't say was I am first nations and I'm a woman. They get to fill two minority spots with one employee; and I get a job. I'll wear my black slacks and white blouse with the crisp black blazer over it. I'll wash and blow dry this to make it soft and pretty." She clawed her fingers through the unfamiliar cap of hair. "I can walk softly in my new leather shoes."

She thought of the pale smoke and how the hunter hides his scent, disguises his spirit, in the fire's breath.

The last of the sun slipped below the edge of the world and night fluttered down like black wings around her. An eerie silence settled. Suddenly she felt she was no longer alone.

"Eagle Dancer?" she whispered. "Eagle Dancer, why have you come?" Silence answered.

"Are you angry too? You accuse me of betrayal! Betrayal of what? Joining the white world? What choice is there left?" She stood on the ledge and raised her open hands to the dark sky above her.

"Eagle Dancer," she cried. "My father and his father and you, Great-Grandfather, you tried to keep the old ways. They don't work anymore! And I'm the one standing here now. I have to save my own life. What is it you want from me?"

Tears rolled down her cold cheeks. "I can't have the old life; it's gone forever. But I can't just safely, quietly wait out my life here, bear children, live off the band…it's not enough. I need to go. I will come back stronger. And I will come back. Marie does not believe me but I will come back."

Lights winked on in the houses on the reserve below. To the east the golden lights of Calgary roared like a golden lion on the horizon.

"Eagle Dancer, give me strength." Dark wings fluttered close with a muffled sound like a heartbeat on the wind. Cool fingers of air whirled around her, through her hair, softy caressing, lifting her heart. The breath of the wind gently dried her tears.

As the stars slipped into the blackening sky she heard a distant coyote howl. Facing east, she lifted her face to the moon and answered him.

Chapter 7
The Gift

(March)

The Greyhound bus from Calgary to Cougar Lake always ran late. It was practically a rule. Sheila sat halfway back on the right hand side as she always did. This way she could see the prairie give way to the grasslands and foothills dotted with lakes as they got closer to home.

But lately all she could see was a great black hole gaping; a whirling vortex from which she was helpless to escape, down which she would spin until the world became empty, black, pinprick small...and then it would simply wink out.

Divorce will do that to you. Especially in a small town. Everyone knew her husband, Brian, had cheated on her. She was pretty sure even the staff and residents at the senior's home where he had worked knew the whole sordid story. Except they knew his version, of course. Not the truth.

The only person Sheila had told her version to was her friend, Janet, and she had sworn Janet to secrecy. It was just too humiliating to have everyone in town know that Brian had been cheating on her for two years and she never once suspected.

This town was the coldest, grayest, wettest place on earth in March. Cold rain had been battering the bus windows since they left Calgary. As they pulled off the #2 Highway the clouds began rolling away to the west. Other passengers wiped the mucky condensation and peered out the windows as the bus rolled through town.

Sheila could see people hurrying along Main Street in the pools of cold, watery sunlight; plodding through the last of the slushy snow. Others wandered in and out of shop doorways. All these people had perfect lives. She knew it. They had perfect, Norman Rockwell families to go home to. It hurt to think about it.

She knew it was time to leave Cougar Lake; leave her home of 30 years, try new cities, new pathways. But her courage was lost somewhere in that oil slick of despair brought into her life by the bitter struggle to emerge from her marriage to Brian. Emerge she had, but so damaged, so empty, even the glory of the surrounding mountains in the last of winter's blaze of crystal snow caps couldn't open her heart as they once would have done.

She dragged her overnight case wearily from the station and went across the street to Cantina's Coffee Stop just to be somewhere else rather than go home to her empty house.

"Hey stranger! Where have you been hiding? I haven't seen you since the Christmas light up event." She looked up. Janet stood at her elbow.

"Hi, Janet," she responded, wishing she didn't have to speak to anyone today. "How are you?" she said, avoiding her friend's question.

Janet put her mocha down on the table and joined Sheila without asking. She began to talk animatedly about her new project, starting a small business in town. She wanted to open a store in the empty building that used to house the second hand store. The store had closed years ago but no one wanted the dusty old space. The "For Lease' sign was so faded you wouldn't know what it said if you hadn't seen it there for years already.

"I think it would be perfect. Rachel Eaglesclaw promised to put me in touch with some of the ladies from the reserve who still do hand crafted leather work. Dara Towers knits those wonderful fingerless gloves and slippers. Tom Wilkes, you know the Mayor's father? Well he still carves the most beautiful wooden birds and other wooden things. There's lots of people make things that I could sell."

Janet's animation was infectious. Sheila began to relax. She realized that as long as the conversation stayed away from her own situation, Brian, and what she was going to do with the rest of her life, she could enjoy the idle chat. But Janet suddenly swung the conversation from idle to full steam ahead.

"So here's the deal," she said. "I run the shop and get the goods. You, my old friend, you handle the legal and business end of things. You could still work at the law office. Our business wouldn't take up all your time. Couldn't pay you anyway, to start. But what a great way to get in on the ground floor of a new enterprise! Whadya say?"

"I don't know, Janet. I don't know what I want to do yet. I'm still in transition."

"Yeah, so help me out while you're transitioning. What have you got to lose?"

"It sounds like it might be fun but really, is Cougar Lake ready for an arts and crafts store? Aren't we a little too country for that?"

"Are you kidding? Look at the folks out there. Yeah, I see cowboy types and farmers but you'd have to be sleep walking not to see the funky element in town. And tourists…the lake draws tourists all summer!"

They watched the people walking past, sprinkling their conversation with funny, nice or nasty comments about the character parade going by on the other side of the window. A young man with curly brown hair and an unshaven face pulled up outside the restaurant in a classic red Chevy, swung into a parking spot barely big enough for the car, and slammed the door as he got out. Sheila was surprised the car could still be in one piece the way he seemed to treat it.

Main Street was always prime real estate for people watching. It wasn't polite or kind, they knew, but it was fun. One of the young men slouching by was wearing the most amazing combination of plaids either of them had ever seen outside a Highlander movie, topped off with a Rasta cap and an old army coat. It cheered Sheila up just to see him.

They left the coffee shop together and went up the street to the Copper Kettle for some lunch. As they sat over grilled chicken salad in taco shell bowls Janet proceeded to redirect the path of Sheila's life. Dropping the business idea in her lap was only the first shot across the bow. She soon fired the second. Without looking up from her salad, Janet tossed a gift in her direction in exactly the off-handed way you might toss a stick of gum to a bothersome child.

"So there's this guy I want you to meet. He's kind and really gentle, very polite. Likes music, likes the outdoors. Very sweet. I met him last summer at that Time Management seminar I went to in Calgary."

Sheila swallowed. "So why don't you date him then?"

"I did. It didn't take."

"Why not?"

"I need more zing, you know?" Janet said.

"Zing?"

"Yah, like I want to be swept off my feet."

"Generally a bad idea to let anyone sweep you anywhere," Sheila replied glumly. "Keep your feet on the ground. That's what I say."

"Ouch. Right. Sorry." Janet licked salsa off her fingers. She watched Sheila methodically stir her tea around and around with a tiny spoon.

"Sooooooo," she said casually, "Do you want to meet him?"

Sheila choked. "Meet him? What do you mean? As in a date? As in a fix-up? As in you want to hand me your used lovers?"

The brightness left Janet's eyes. She glared at Sheila. "As in, if you want to meet him I'll give him your number. If you don't, I won't. That's all! I take no responsibility for what happens after that! All I'm doing is providing an introduction. And you're welcome!"

"I'm sorry, Janet, really," Sheila said. "I guess you just took me by surprise. I thought you were telling me about him because you were getting back together." She reached out and squeezed her friend's hand. "Sorry, Janet. I'm just really grumpy these days. And it's way, way too soon to be even thinking about men. If I ever do again." She grimaced.

"It's okay. I get it. But first of all he's NOT my lover," said Janet. "And I'm not interested. He's nice, but he's just separated from his wife, not even divorced yet. So in that sense you two would be perfect for each other. Just someone to go out with, you know? Nothing serious or anything."

Sheila stopped the forkful of salad halfway to her lips. "What? He's still married?" She clanged her fork down on the table. "Then I am for sure not interested! At least I'm divorced."

A scruffy looking man in a dirty baseball cap stared at them from another table. Janet raised her eyebrows and stared back. He quickly looked away.

"Well he's filed for divorce and been living on his own for 6 months now. He told me that much. I told him I just don't want to wait for some guy to get his divorce finalized. I want some action now."

"You're weird, girlfriend," Sheila told her. "You'll keep seeing men, one after another, like beads on a string, waiting for instant intimacy but you won't wait for a divorce to be finalized."

"It's not that, I just don't want a man on the rebound."

"But it's okay for me?"

"I didn't mean it that way."

"Well, your loss. From all you've told me so far he sounds pretty perfect, other than the divorce thing."

"Well, he's not perfect, exactly," Janet mumbled around a mouthful.

"Okay, what's the catch?!!" Sheila demanded.

"No catch. It's just that I know the kind of guys you used to go out with, you know, before. Charming, funny, smart. He's kind of, well, quiet. Ordinary. A blue jean and T-shirt kind of guy."

"Oh oh. This does not sound good."

"It's not bad," Janet continued quickly. "He's just not what you're used to. You were used to Brian and he was pretty high end, if you know what I mean, that's all. Always in a suit, always dressed to the nine's, always with money. You know, big city guys?"

"But didn't you say this guy lives in Calgary?"

"Well, yeah," Janet said. "But he could fit in fine out here in Cougar Lake too."

"Oh brother," Sheila moaned. "I don't know, Janet. Now he's starting to sound like all the redneck fools we went to high school with and couldn't get away from fast enough. Besides, I'm not sure I even want to stay here in Alberta anymore."

"You know what. Just give it a chance. You're up in Calgary

next week on assignment again, aren't you? Just go for coffee. What can it hurt?"

"All right. But he probably feels about women right now the way I feel about men."

"Ah, Honey. You'll get over that. Trust me."

They finished their lunch in silence. Sheila was working through a thousand questions: What if, by ordinary, she means unattractive? What if, by quiet, she means he's got nothing intelligent to say? And...What if he's still hung-up on his ex-wife? Or worse yet, on Janet? Do I want to even meet a man who comes as a gift from someone else? It's like being given a hand-me down dress. No, that's not fair. The guy's a human being not a possession, but still...

"I guess any man I meet at this stage in life is going to be a hand-me down from some other woman," she said aloud.

"Yeah but don't forget," Janet grinned at her, "We're a hand-me-down woman from a previous man too, right?

"I never looked at it that way."

They got up and cleared their dishes, waved to the waitress and left the restaurant. Without comment they both automatically turned at Pender St. to walk the two blocks down to the lake. It was always nicer to walk home along the lake shore trail.

"I don't know, Janet. Maybe I should keep trying to meet someone on my own? I could try internet dating."

Janet squinted her eyes and puckered her lips like she had just swallowed a jalapeno pepper. "I never had any luck with that. They were all jerks. Just looking for sex. Besides at least this one's been pre-screened; at least you know he's not an axe-murderer. What harm is there in meeting for a cup of coffee?"

"Okay, but what if we click majorly and then spend the rest of our lives dealing with embarrassment because he and my best friend once were an item?"

"Oh Sheila. Grow up!" Janet's frustration sizzled. "Take a leap in the dark for a change!"

"Okay. Jeez."

"What?"

"I said yes. I would appreciate it if you would give Neil my number."

"Whew. Okay, but remember, whatever happens it's NOT my fault."

"Deal."

As they walked Sheila noticed the rain had stopped. Cold, crisp sunlight was sparkling on the dripping trees and the puddles on the path. The hills on the far side of the lake flickered with watery golden light and long shadows stretched up the slopes. *Probably why I feel a hell of a lot better than I did an hour ago, she thought. That and a good lunch.*

"Are you sure you're all right with this?" she asked. "I mean if you're giving him up for me, that's a gift I can't accept."

"No, it's okay," Janet grinned. "Besides, I've got another one lined up already."

"You witch! You're incredible!"

Janet laughed. She turned off the path and headed toward her apartment. Sheila stood for a moment and watched a long-legged heron tiptoe quietly in the shallows. The trees all around her were still jeweled from the rain. She breathed deeply, inhaling the silence, then turned up the next street to the office where she worked as a legal aid for one of Cougar Lake's two lawyers, Mayor Wilkes' husband.

She wondered if she would have been able to do the same for Janet. Even if a relationship is over it would be hard to see him with another woman. She couldn't bear the thought of Brian... *No,* she thought. *I am simply not going there!*

The next day, she stood and looked out her office window

across the little stand of trees in the green space opposite. Those trees had been young and flexible enough to survive the massive wind storm that swept away a lot of the town's older trees in 2005. Luckily the town hadn't been hit with anything like that since.

The phone rang. "Sheila MacPherson?" a deep, mellow voice asked. "It's Neil. Janet's friend?"

Suddenly she felt out of place in her quiet office. She struggled for a moment in that twilight displacement between professional and personal lives; like over-lapping ripples on the water, the lines become blurred.

"I wasn't expecting to hear from you so soon," she blurted. "Janet only told me about you yesterday."

"Ah," said the voice. "Well, she's been telling me about you for months."

"Really?"

They agreed to meet for coffee; a quick and harmless meeting in a neutral locale in Calgary the following Tuesday when Sheila would be working in the city.

On Tuesday, as the bus rolled north, it occurred to her the city looked like a rather lonely island of grey monoliths standing out from the surrounding prairie, isolated. When she was in the city it never felt like that. It felt like the city environment simply was the entire world.

As she walked toward the downtown core that evening, the Centre Street lions welcomed her into a world that shimmered with more light and promise than the city had offered in a long time. The Stephen Avenue Mall glowed down its length with antique light standards gracefully curving over the street.

Sheila slowed as she approached the café on the mall where they had agreed to meet. Outside the coffee shop, amid the whirl of theatre-goers, bright lights and confusion, stood an island of tranquility. A tall, gentle looking man calmly surveying the crowds flowing past. From Janet's description it could be no-one else. He was 6' tall, large and slightly rounded, with thick grey hair gently lifting in the cold wind. His hands were buried in his coat pockets. He was not hunk material, certainly.

Actually he looks really boring. I could just walk by. Pretend I never got here.

She stopped and just watched him for a moment.

Then again, I've been married to a man who was too good-looking to be faithful; charming and clever in public but hard and cold and angry in private; someone so high voltage I was slowly being drained of my own power. Maybe boring might be good for a while.

She took a deep breath and walked up to him. "Hi, are you Neil?"

His hazel eyes met hers and he smiled slowly.

"I am indeed," he said. "Nice to finally meet you."

"Nice to meet you, too." Brilliant conversational opener, she thought.

Neil just smiled. "Shall we go in?" He held the door for her. Obviously on his best first date behaviour.

They sat with steaming bowls of cappuccino and began to ask and answer all the usual questions two strangers ask each other. He seemed genuinely interested in her answers. Not just waiting to get a chance to talk about himself. *A refreshing change from Brian.* she admitted to herself.

Before she knew it, they were closing the cafe four hours, two chocolate chip muffins and several more cappuccinos later. As they walked back together across Prince's Island, Neil took her hand without comment and she suddenly felt safer in the darkness with him than she did alone in broad daylight. On Memorial Drive the street lights seemed to shimmer in bright silver, green and pale blues.

At the apartment she shared when she came into the city, they made more coffee neither of them wanted and talked of all the things they loved: dogs, music, walking, theatre, the outdoors and opera. At 2:00 a.m. they made sandwiches while Andrea Bocelli filled the air with the glory of Puccini. Oddly the apartment seemed filled with soft colour and light as well as music. And then she realized this man she had never met before was standing by her side actually slicing cheese, buttering bread and washing coffee cups. Her husband hadn't done these things in 18 years of marriage.

When they finally said goodnight a lavender dawn was touching the top of Bankers Hall in the distance. Its pinnacles looked, from her window, like an enchanted castle. The light slowly bloomed outward and covered the skyline of the city in rainbows of colour.

The following morning she watched the city slip past the Greyhound bus windows. The first shy green leaves were a still curled hint of spring to come. The recent rains left a sparkle of silver over everything. Buildings stood out sharply against a luminous blue sky and windows everywhere caught the morning sun.

She tried to move her mind from him to the work waiting at the office in Cougar Lake but a dozen times in as many minutes came the little jolts of uncertainty. She wanted to take him apart to see how he worked; to see if there was someone under the surface who might actually mean something in her life. She stared out the window at the flat cerulean sky. Her cell phone rang as they were passing through High River. When she opened her phone she heard his rich baritone voice.

"Good morning. I just heard the weather report for the weekend. It's supposed to be beautiful. I called to see if you might want to go for a spring hike this weekend in Banff?"

What a peculiar choice for a second date, she thought. No fancy dinner, no dancing, no movie; just a walk on a woodland trail. As he spoke, the bus roof became a canopy of sunlit branches; she could see the feathered shadows of trees flickering on the ceiling; could smell the scent of pine in the air and hear the squeaky chirping of curious Gray Jays in the tree tops.

As a child she had loved hiking and camping with her family. Living in Cougar Lake, so close to the mountains, her family had done a lot of wilderness outings together. As a woman she put such things away locked in a box of memory. How odd that this ordinary man should have the key.

Maybe what she needed was someone like this; someone with a sweet smile, a voice like a wind through a canyon. Nothing fancy, just a kind and simple heart. In the distance the clouds settled down on the mountain tops like a mother robin fluffing her feathers about her chicks.

"I'd love to," she said.

Chapter 8
The Boy Who Tried To Lose
(April)

A slow moving procession of two moved along the lake shore. It was Wednesday and the boy should have been in school but "should have" played no appreciable part in his life. Instead he played with the waves as they chased him, ran up to him, then dashed away in playful haste, leaving a wet lick along his ankles. The early spring wind brought a froth of white caps to Cougar Lake.

The old woman followed some way behind; bow-legged, bent and softly sagging. She wore bright green slacks that glowed fluorescent against pale, white ankles. She dragged a rough sack behind her in the dirt.

The boy ran back from time to time to drop his findings into the sack then dashed away to search among faded logs. His crow-black hair and golden skin seemed more at home here, among the rocky headlands and wind-brushed pines than did the faded shadow of the woman.

She stopped and called to him. They sat together, facing the blue-grey expanse of the lake in the way of all people in the presence of water. She pulled a battered thermos from the sack. Steam erupted into the cool air. She handed the cup to the boy and he swallowed the hot tea in quick little gulps then was off to the shoreline again. The woman remained staring out at the line of pale light where water and sky faded together.

The clouds formed silver roads on the sky. Mist clothed the mountains and hills behind her in primordial cloaks.

She poured her tea; her hands, pale bird's claws, clutched the cup to her lips. Her ragged hair was the gray of faded seaweed and as coarse and confused. There was a rhythm to the twitching of her head that followed an ancient music. The skin of her face hung in waves between cheekbone and nose. The pale eyes were the heart of a flower radiating petals of flesh.

A pale old woman and a golden boy...two figures in a landscape, sharing only isolation and a mug of tea. But they shared a silence, too, that told of time spent together and understanding; a safe and easy distance from the world of others. An internal radar tuned so delicately to each other's movements that, when the old woman rose and packed away the thermos, the boy's meanderings took on the same direction, without a glance, as the progress she made westward into shadows that now began to strafe the beach in lines of bright and dark. Soon the trail of the bag began leaving deeper and deeper ruts beside two sets of footprints, side by side, in the dirt.

The boy had tried to get her to play the "catch me" game today but even earlier when the bag was light she wouldn't play. It worried him. He ran back to her with a dirty glass bottle that still had the cap attached. A rare find.

"Look, Grandma" he cried. "We can use this, can't we?"

"Rinse it and put it in the sack," she said. There was no answering smile. Before she would have smiled her toothless grin at him but lately she wouldn't. He ran to the water and rinsed the bottle. His cold, wet fingers slid the bottle carefully into the sack. He stood beside her for a moment. He no longer looked up into her face. He had grown big enough over the past winter to meet her eye to eye.

She shook her head and turned her face away.

The curve of the bay ended in jumbled rock where small trapped pools writhed with life: fresh water clams, water spiders, minnows, frogs, snails. Among the brush slithered the little striped bodies of garter snakes. The boy gently reached out to touch a snake that was curled up and sunning itself. The snake instantly uncoiled and zipped into the undergrowth. The boy glanced up with a guilty grin. The old woman scowled.

"I've told you. You don't touch. Even watching a living creature can harm it."

"I know," he said, "Sorry."

Many times she had told him to leave alone a small bird or animal when all he was doing was watching it. Part of him understood. He knew how uncomfortable he felt in town when other children stared. It hurt. Not in any physical way but with a feeling of being unsafe, vulnerable. So the creatures of Cougar Lake were safe from him. He watched them with care to learn how they moved, how they lived, what they ate, where they slept, but he left if they showed the slightest unease.

The old woman was having trouble now scrambling over the rocks but he didn't go back to help her. He had learned to wander at his own pace and let her struggle along at hers. Although it worried him that her pace was so much slower now. He worried that she might simply blow away one day in the strong winds that often raged down from the north in the winter. Her old gray sweater hung from her shoulders over a faded plaid shirt. She wore two pairs of men's pants, one over the other for warmth.

Her home sat up a long dirt track that left the main road from town and meandered up to a level clearing. Her closest neighbour was a 15 minute walk up the road. He was a single man, graying but still strong, who lived in a derelict mobile home that he had renovated and turned into a solid living space. His only companion was a massive gentle sheep dog who never left his side. He kept pretty much to himself but he could be counted on to help in an emergency.

A few years ago the owner of the motel in town where her daughter had been staying had called to say her daughter was gone and she needed to come pick up the little boy. It was her neighbour, Paul, who drove her to town. She found her grandson alone in the motel room amongst a litter of bottles, junk food wrappers and broken needles.

The tiny cabin they now shared was heated by a wood fire and lit with oil lamps or candles. They gathered wood washed up on the beach or deadfall from the forest. In winter he had to lay it out to dry before it would burn. It disappeared unimaginably quickly for all his work. In addition to the wood, they gathered snails and forest tubers, mushrooms, and berries later in the season. Sometimes they fished for rainbow trout.

They usually made a trip to the town campground on Mondays when the campers had all left and they could scrounge for food, broken bits of cooking gear, anything useful left by the tourists. Sometimes they even found toys that had been left behind and those were his favorite days. A found toy was a treasure that made him laugh with delight.

Today the bag was very full and this, he knew, would make her happy. Tomorrow was the day they would walk to town for her government pension and some groceries. She would buy them lunch: a treat of sweet buns, cheese and fruit. They would eat in the park, leaving crumbs for the pigeons.

But now she was beckoning to him, an irritated wag of a crooked finger, and they moved deeper into the forest, away from the sighing green waves. Above, the high grey sky was sprinkled with clouds, drifting like icing sugar across glass. He imagined climbing into the green canopy above and sticking out his tongue to taste the clouds.

He clambered up a small rise and looked out over the lake to the far shore where he knew the cougars roamed. When he looked around, she was gone. She could walk more silently than anyone. Her worn shoes, laced with string, padded over the underbrush like cat's paws. He ran to catch her.

Suddenly, a gnarled hand grabbed his shoulder and pointed down through the wood toward a small inlet. A blue heron stood on one long leg. Slender, crested head motionless. As they watched, the boneless neck suddenly uncoiled and flew silently into the water, emerging with a graceful silver flash of fish.

Further on she found a bed of small spring mushrooms. He picked just enough to fry for their supper, leaving plenty for the forest. While he picked she spoke to him.

In a rusty voice she said, "There was a time I didn't know the shapes and colours right. I picked some bad ones. And ate them. I was awful sick. I couldn't get right no matter what I did. I walked up the road to Paul's and he took me to the doctor. Doctor gave me some medicine that smelled like piss. Just smelling the stuff made me vomit so when I got home I threw it away. Felt a whole lot better right away."

He laughed but she scowled at him. As long as he had lived with her, she had never been sick. But he remembered long nights of fever when the old hands had soothed the hot skin of his forehead; forced him to sip teas that tasted of fields and meadows; curled against him in the small bed to still his shivering.

If they loved each other it was because of those dark, sad nights and the long, yellow days. He knew she would have preferred to be left in peace in her quiet woodland home. He understood that. He didn't understand why his mother never came back for him. At first he asked about his mother; cried himself to sleep missing her. His grandmother wouldn't talk about her and eventually he stopped asking. He only knew she shared her home and meager food with him. She cared for him and taught him to live in the only world she knew.

Smoky memories of the world before still slept within him though, like the glimmer of a candle in the distance. He lived with two worlds, in uneasy peace, inside him. The world of his mother: parties, friends, men, moving constantly from place to place. The world of his grandmother: the quiet stillness of the forest, food they grew or gathered, chess by the fire, the same roof above him each morning.

When they got home the trap-injured fox was limping around inside the makeshift cage. He fed the fox then gathered a few potatoes and carrots from the covered hole that served as their root cellar. They sat in the feeble light of the single oil lamp and ate their supper of potatoes, carrots and mushrooms, fried and fragrant, and the last crust of bread. Tomorrow they would be rich again. Afterward he arranged the plates and pan outside the door for the raccoons. He would wash them in the morning.

When darkness had settled in, sliding up from the lake and swallowing the hillside, a sweep of bright light shone through the trees as a big red car roared up the road. It stopped in front of the cabin. The boy ran out to the car.

"Hey Buddy," Matt said as he handed the boy a carton of eggs through the window.

"Hi Matt," the boy said shyly. He ran his hands lovingly over the sleek lines of the Chevelle. His finger traced the clumps of marshmallow still glued to one window. "I could help you wash it sometime," he offered.

"I just might take you up on that, Kid. Don't forget. I'm going to teach you to drive it when you're old enough."

The boy's face split in a huge grin. He waved goodbye as Matt peeled away.

After he put the eggs in the cold storage he got out the tattered chess board and laid it on the floor before the hearth. His chocolate eyes softly watched as the old woman knelt and fed the fire. They played without speaking. As usual, she won, laughing her magpie's harsh chuckle. He was silent.

He had cheated. He had seen a chance to put her in check and, although excited by the idea, had deliberately not taken it. There had been a moment of fierce pride when he saw that he could finally beat her. Then the fear swept into his heart. He feared the winning. He knew it had to come sometime but he feared it. When he won, it would be the end. She would leave him then, he was sure. He would be alone to gather the wood and mushrooms, to plant the potatoes and carrots and harvest them. To catch fish in the lake and to play chess alone at night. How empty the cabin would be. He dreaded not hearing the hiss of the oil lamp outside his bedroom at night.

The memory of his mother crept in that night like a stealthy mouse, gnawing at his heart. If his grandmother left him like his mother had, what would he do?

He would survive, he supposed. He wouldn't go hungry. The snails were here. He knew how to catch the Northern Pike, Walleye and RTrout that swam in the lake. He had the garden. But he didn't know how she got the government cheque every month. Paul might know. He would go to him. He was a grown up. He would help him. Paul lived all alone too with only his enormous sheepdog for company. That's what he would do. He could get a dog.

Yes, he would be all right but he would miss the old woman.

Miss her silence and her hobbling gait. Miss the touch of her rustling fingers, like dry leaves, as they smoothed back the hair from his eyes. Maybe, after the winter snows had come and gone once more, maybe he would try again to win...just once. And maybe he was wrong. It might be that nothing would happen at all. But once before it had happened.

Once before there was warmth and light and loud, laughing voices after he was curled in bed. His mother and her friends; always different friends. Then the nights when it was just the two of them and they would play Go Fish with the animal cards. They would play on the big bed with the flowered quilt. His mother always won because she always pretended she didn't have the animal he asked for. She would win and she would laugh and take some more medicine from her bottle. He didn't mind losing because at least she was playing with him.

When they drove all the way from Vancouver to stay here at the lake and visit his grandmother his Mom started getting sadder and angrier. He didn't like it. He didn't like the old motel they had to stay in either. It smelled.

Then one night when they played she seemed sleepy and not really trying. He had one card left. He knew she had the match. He slapped it on the bed.

"I won," he cried. He remembered dancing wildly around the room.

"Don't be so damn proud! I just LET you win," she said.

Maybe she let him win that night, maybe not. He didn't know. And maybe it had nothing to do with what happened later. But to his small-child mind everything that night seemed tied with that first time of winning and his joy at having beaten his mother and his mother's anger at having been beaten by a little kid!

His pride had been great that night and he dreamed...of

being alone...being all powerful...controlling the very winds and the movements of the moon.

In the morning he woke hungry, crying and alone. He cried and watched the light grow, then fade. He wet himself in his desperation and still no one came to smack him for it. He screamed and threw himself against the wooden door again and again with painful thuds.

Finally the door opened and the old woman stood there, haloed by headlights. He was too exhausted and hungry to even cry. Silently she picked him up, carried him to a truck and took him home.

He remembered nothing more from that time except vague images of darkness and fear. The old woman could tell him little more, only that she did not know where his mother was and didn't really care.

"She made her bed. She can lie in it," was all she said.

When he grew as tall as the children who caught the school bus, he asked her where they went.

"They go to a place of foolishness," she said. "A place where children learn to be foolish and ugly and mean. Your mother would have sent you. It's the law and she didn't need any more trouble with the law. But the law never did me no good so why should I do what they say?" She snorted and spat at this. He dared ask nothing more.

From then on he hid when the yellow bus rolled by. He would peek out and watch as it passed; listen in fascination to the clamour of children Sometimes someone came to talk with her and she made him hide in the root cellar. The voices, drifting like strange snow through the wall, would ask many questions.

"He's only here for a visit," she would say. "My daughter has him registered at school back in Vancouver."

Or "He's gone. My daughter came back and got him."

The old woman would not answer any more questions and the strange voices became angry and left. He would catch a glimpse of white hands opening shining car doors; thin, angry hands.

Sometimes he still dreamed of the before time. He saw the pink and blue flowers on the quilt. He was drinking soda pop while his mother drank from her bottle. They were playing cards and laughing. Then he won the game. His mother became angry and started to throw the animal cards into his face. The wild winds started howling. They crashed through the windows. A roaring, whirling darkness. Stinging rain. The rain was sticky and smelled of her medicine. In the swirling blackness she was gone. He would wake up screaming. His Grandmother held him when he woke and gently wiped his face. His face and hands felt dirty.

In the morning he would swim in the cool of the lake to make himself clean. Or, if the lake water was too cold or iced over, he would splash stinging icy water from the stream that ran down behind the cabin; the stream that provided their fresh water summer and winter.

But now, in the silence of the forest days, he was clean. Now, in the silence of the old woman's home, he was safe. He could never leave to face the dreams alone. He could never bear it if she left him. And so he knew ... he must never win when they played chess. It would be too terrible if it all happened again. Maybe he could win the game and nothing would happen... maybe. But there was still that frightened little child inside him that still believed in the power... the power that had made his mother go away once before. A child's power to make things happen by believing in them.

No, he must never, never win!

And he must hide from her the fact that he could.

For as long as he could.

Chapter 9
The Name Of Morning
(May)

It was unusually early for the only taxi in town to be out and working, but when Sandra called him from the Greyhound station he said he would just finish his coffee and be right there. Her single suitcase fit on the seat beside her. Few of the stores along Main Street had unlocked their doors yet but the coffee shops and cafes were open for breakfast.

As the taxi made its way toward the end of Harold Street where she was headed, they passed an old woman and a small boy dragging a large sack behind them. They flinched and stepped off the street into the trees when the taxi passed.

That's odd. I don't recognize either of them. Maybe I've been gone longer than I thought.

The taxi dropped her at the end of the muddy lane leading to her house. She could just see the edge of the cornflower tinted siding. The house was almost hidden by the stand of birch in spring lime-green. A battered red car was parked up the road. She thought she recognized it but surely it's owner was an old man not the scruffy young man sitting in it playing a harmonica? Just another memory that did not fit reality.

The early morning sunlight drew bars of gold and black across the lane. Water droplets from the morning's rain glistened on leaves and grass blades and dampened the toes of her suede boots. It seemed strange to be here and yet eerily familiar.

It was like so many other fleeting glimpses that came and went in her imagination. She thought of these visions like the flash of a cheetah through a forest. Strange but fleeting. Not real.

Often the visions felt like being back home here in Cougar Lake. But always the town, the lake and the surrounding layers of blue foothills and green forests would flash out of existence and she would be back in the dining hall at the hospital.

The odd thing was this time she actually felt the cool dampness and could smell the freshness of the grass as the blades bruised beneath her feet. She truly saw the dark edge of moisture crawling up her boots with each step. It seemed real. She could even hear the orchestra of frogs from the nearby creek that ran through the property.

What time was it now? Six am? Seven? The sun was up but the shadows were still angled long across the grass. An odd time of day to be coming home. But then everything has been odd for so long.

She was dressed in a thick cobalt blue sweater and black jeans so obviously she was not coming home from an all-night party. From work then? No, it wasn't likely she would be dressed like this at work and certainly not coming home at this time of the morning.

Then she remembered the taxi and turned quickly to look behind her. The taxi was gone. She had walked this far. She tried to look like she knew what she was doing. She lengthened her stride and lifted her head and walked toward the house. Her house. It was her house, wasn't it?

There was smoke, a thin silver thread, fluttering from the chimney. It drifted down over the dark blue tiled roof. Erupting pigeons startled up from the grass and flew beyond the trees.

I wonder what they'll say when they see me walk in. Have I been gone a long time? I feel as though I should have more luggage if I've been away on a trip. I must have forgotten it somewhere.

Her feet crunched up the path; small red stones ran like a brook up to the porch. The wood on the porch was starting to rot in places.

I'll have to get some scrap pieces from that guy at the lumber yard up the highway and fix that. What was his name? I used to have him in for coffee whenever he came by to deliver wood for the hen house or stain for the fence. Now I can't remember what to call him. Not that it matters really. If I just smile and say Hi he'll assume I remember. Same with the others.

She could hear them inside the house now. A little girl was talking loudly. Much too loudly. She should be reminded that girls are gentle and do not shout. Her own mother had rubbed burning soap into her mouth if she talked too loudly or sassed. It frothed and foamed and left a bitter taste against her tongue and lips. Mother would shove the soap bar deep into her mouth until she could feel the corners pressing against the back of her throat and she would gag.

She told the doctors her mother was trying to kill her. Her mother said it was to teach her to watch her mouth and keep properly quiet. She learned. And when the doctors tried to get her to talk about her feelings she could taste that dark, bitter soap. She kept quiet.

The door opened suddenly and a small body thumped into hers. The startled child looked up then backed away out of the crisp sunlight.

"Um, hello," she said to the child. She stuffed her hands in her pockets and tried to look casual, as if it was a perfectly ordinary thing to be standing on this porch at this time of morning. The sounds of rattling dishes and a barking dog formed a wall of sound in the doorway as effective as any solid door. The little girl stared.

"Daddy," the girl called without turning her head. "Daddy!" This time it came out two tones higher.

Sandra tried to smile at the girl but she could feel the smile was ragged at the edges and probably looked more like a grimace.

"It's Mommy!" The girl tilted her head to get this information back into the kitchen without taking her eyes off Sandra.

"Were you just leaving for school, Sweetheart?" Without a name to attach to this girl, Sweetheart would have to do for now. She thought maybe she should try to hug the girl but she was standing in the doorway on sturdy, spread legs.

How do you go about it anyway? Who initiates a hug? Don't they just happen? And how do I hug someone who only stands as tall as my last rib?

Then all of a sudden there was a man hugging her. A wet dish towel hung from his hand and draped across her shoulder. She stared at its stains. He felt big and warm and smelled wonderful: a mixture of coffee, bacon, smoke, sweaty shirts, and dish soap. How wonderful that this man should want to hug her. Sandra smiled at the girl over his shoulder. A real smile this time.

"I'm so glad you're home, Honey. Why didn't you tell us you were coming? I could have picked you up." When he stepped back to look at her, his eyes were a little wary but she could tell he wanted to be happy to see her. And he looked straight into her eyes. That was startling. The doctors never looked you in the eye. They asked their questions looking out windows and heard the answers bent over notebooks. The nurses, when they talked to you, looked at whatever it was they were doing, not at you.

"I took the first bus out this morning," she said. "Got the

taxi from the station. I'm sorry. I'm disturbing your routine."

"No. Jeez. Don't say that. You live here too you know?"

"Sometimes," she said stupidly.

"Come have some coffee with me," he said. "It's chilly out here."

He put an arm around her shoulders and then she found herself sitting in a cluttered blue and white kitchen. How eerily familiar; like a photograph looked at so many times it becomes more real than the original scene. It felt like being back in a dream that she had almost succeeded in forgetting.

"Where's all your stuff?" he asked. "I thought they were releasing you this weekend. The kids and I were going to drive up and pick you up. "

"It's still there. They said I could leave it. Maybe…well… we can all drive up together some time to get it?" He seemed disappointed so she said this as cheerfully as she could, trying to make it sound like a fun excursion. In reality the thought of anything more future than the next minute was beyond her.

"So are you…I mean…this is it?" he asked. "They don't need you back?"

She shook her head without knowing quite what he meant. *Who would want me back? Who needs me? I'm just a figment of my own imagination. An empty shell. I'm 36, or so it says on my birth certificate but I don't believe it. If I'm 36 why am I just as stupid and lost as I was at 16? Thirty six is mature. An adult. An adult was someone who always knew what to do and say. Someone in control. Someone you went to if you were lost or injured.*

"Where is…?" *If I don't try so hard the names will come.* "Where's the boy? I should say hello."

The man looked curiously at her for a moment then said,

"Of course, Honey. I'm sorry. He's collecting the eggs. I'll call him in." The man, the husband, the person who sent her there but who also came to see her every week without fail.

He stuck his head out the door and yelled into the crisp spring morning. "C'mon in here, son. Your Mother's home."

Mother. The word burned on her ears. But of course it must be true because there was her daughter, still standing on the other side of the table, staring at her with eyes as blue as hers had once been. And there, coming in the door, was her son. A tall, loose-limbed sort of boy in overalls over his school clothes.

Do children still wear those? Do they still do the chores before school? I know I did but that seems so long ago and things have changed so much and none of it makes any sense.

The boy put down the straw lined bucket filled with thin brown eggs. He walked slowly across the floor toward her. Sandra could see his father standing behind him, smiling, nodding encouragingly to her.

What? What? Am I supposed to do something? I've forgotten my lines.

Dr. Walker had said, "Just let it come naturally. Don't rush it. The fears will still be there but you mustn't let them sweep you away. You can control your reactions. Don't let them control you."

But Dr. Walker, I don't know this thin, scruffy person standing here. Maybe I knew his name once but…wait…yes. Yes I still do.

"Hello Kevin." She had given him that name. Her first baby. Named for the black orderly in the hospital during Kevin's birth. The one who covered her with a warm blanket. He spoke so softly to her as she lay in the hallway waiting in a stream of groaning, screaming women. It had all been so frightening. So terribly different than what she had expected.

The face and gentle voice she remembered most from those long, dreadful hours was a face as black as coffee and a name tag: Kevin.

I've never told my son. Maybe I will someday.

His smile was shy but at least he knew her. He came to her and put his arms around her awkwardly then touched his cold cheek to hers.

"Don't cry, Mom. You're home now," he said.

Startled, she reached up to touch her cheek and was surprised to find it wet. His cheek, too, was wet where it had touched hers. She used to translate tears into anger. Hide them beneath a cloud of fury. It seemed the stronger of the two choices. Now they were as natural to her as urinating. She had gotten used to them. She couldn't very long be ashamed of tears in that place with everyone so troubled themselves and always the people creeping in soft white shoes.

Things slowly remembered themselves behind her eyes. The avocado plant in the window, dead now. It had started as an experiment for school and had turned into a battle ground when the care was handed, as everything always was, to her. The star-shaped scar on her daughter's forehead where she hit the dresser, trying to climb out of her crib. Sandra had been too tired to answer her cries. Always too tired.

"Pauline." She turned to the little girl, certain now she had the name right. It was the only name that fit that round, pink face framed in her own dark curls. She was born with the morning sun. She needed a cheerful, morning name to counteract her mother's dark pain. A cheerful, pink name.

"Pauline? Are you glad to have me home?"

Pauline looked to her father and Sandra caught his frown.

He has coached them! I'm the enemy here. They're the family.

"Remember," Dr. Walker said. "They've been struggling

along without you for almost two years. They'll have developed their own routines and habits. Children can change a great deal in that time. You must understand their hesitancy to welcome you back. It's not you, but the change they fear. They'll be wary. Give them time. And give yourself time to adjust."

Doctors. Theories. What did he know of being a mother or a woman in this world? What could he feel of the agony of that kind of responsibility? That kind of power? The power to hurt these babies. To strap them to chairs to correct their posture. To make them fetch the belt for whippings. I remember once after Mother whipped me I vomited and the tears and the vomit ran down my clothes. I was forced to stay in those filthy clothes. The rest of the memory is dark, and lonely and hungry. Dr. Walker made a big thing of it when I finally told him.

"Pauline, it's okay," she managed to say. "I understand. I'm sort of like a stranger right now and you're not sure you can trust me. Right?" Pauline was on the other side of the table, hands in pockets, mouth puckered as if full of marbles.

"Pauline?" Mark said quietly. He stood wiping a dish that had long since dried. His hands were work-red and he looked tired.

"I guess so," she said. The smooth varnished table, littered with plates and smudgy jam jars, rattled between them as she kicked at a table leg with a small, sneakered foot. Sandra tried to shut out the noise and not scream.

It's so hard to get used to child noises again. Where are the clean, pastel rooms and the quietly shining floors? Where is my crisp white bed and the quiet white shoes? So peaceful and safe. But they told me to go home. To you, Pauline. To your child sounds. And yet…I remember your laughter. Your tears. Your sweet voice calling me to come see the new kitten in the barn; talking with words tumbling upside down in your joy. Silent, pale walls and cushioned shoes never brought those living noises.

"Is it okay then? Can we be friends for a while?" Sandra asked.

"I dunno. Are you really gonna stay home this time?" Pauline kicked harder at the table leg, still looking down behind a wall of falling curls.

"I'm back for good now, Sweetheart. If that's what you and Kevin and Daddy want." Her husband stood at the sink with the dish towel in his hands.

"You're not…afraid of us anymore?" It was almost a whisper.

A blaze of pain went through her head at these words. She expected Mark to step in and slap the girl. She rose to stop him. Hand out, fingers splayed. But he just stood at the sink, watching. Waiting. His heavy fingers with a worn gold band rested on Kevin's young shoulder. The kitchen door was slightly open behind him and the birch trees lining the drive beckoned into a dreaming distance. It was so clean and open and quiet out there in the sun.

"You live in a small town," Dr. Walker had said. "It will be hard for people not to talk about where you've been. They'll be curious. You don't owe them any explanations. You've been ill, that's all. Keep in mind that you, and you alone, control the conversation."

I could just go back. It doesn't matter. They've been doing just fine without a wife and mother. And I never claimed to be either one so why not?

Pauline looked up at her then. Her blue eyes round with fear.

Because, Mother, I'm not you. And I never will be. That's why.

"Sweetheart, I wasn't afraid of you. Never of you. It was me I was afraid of. But I won't be anymore. I promise."

"C'mon Pauly. Lighten up," Kevin said, moving closer. Her little knight in shining armour.

She willed herself to step around the table to Pauline. But her daughter backed away. Nausea reeled through her. She gripped the nausea tightly and knelt down on the floor. She held her arms open, just a little, hands gently cupped. Pauline shuffled, then came, proud and grudging. Her hair was soft and warm as kitten fur against Sandra's cheek.

She looked up to find Mark smiling a huge, warm smile. It lifted the strain from around his eyes. Hesitantly she smiled back over their daughter's head. She couldn't help noticing his hair was greyer than it used to be.

How hard this must be for him. How hard the last two years doing this all alone. For him then. For Mark. And for these two beautiful children. For them I'll stay, at least for a while.

Chapter 10
Please Take Her Violets
(June)

The old man spoke through the gaps in his ragged teeth. "Nicole? D'you have a minute?" He was plucking with stiff, tobacco stained fingers at the cigar ash dusting the front of his shirt. "I really need to talk to somebody. Somebody needs to listen to me. Nobody here seems to have time to listen. Please?"

"You've been out in the yard smoking again, haven't you, Mr. Harrison?" Nicole was doing her evening rounds as usual. She was heavily pregnant now and waddled in the corridors like a penguin. She would be on maternity leave starting next week.

She was used to the old man's rambling. Sometimes she actually enjoyed listening to him although she couldn't usually stay long. She wheeled his chair over beside the bed and began to turn down the sheets and set up the bed pan for the night.

"People laugh at me when I try to tell them about the old days and the war. You've heard of Ypres or Verdun?"

"I have," she said.

"Well most folks have no time for such things now. Most people don't even remember reading about the Great War in their history books, much less really remember it. But I do. And not just the war," he let her help him out of the chair and onto the edge of the bed. "I remember everything. Not just the war. Before the war. The swish of the girls skirts on wooden floors at the dances. Root beer floats at the old drug store. God they were good! I miss those. I was young then; young as you are now."

"Take my arm, Mr. Harrison. Let's get you settled in."

He touched her hand with gnarled fingers. "I remember the touch of my daughter's hand; the feel of her little fingers in mine when we went out for walks together."

Nicole propped the pillows up behind his head and smoothed the few strands of white hair that stood up like tiny sheaves of wheat behind his ears. Matt made fun of Mr. Harrison because of the way he looked but Nicole liked him. He was at least interesting to talk to.

"What?" he asked. "You smiled just then. You think I'm a funny old man with my ragged teeth and the ashes always falling on my shirt and all this ugly, wrinkled skin. And these," he held up trembling fingers, swollen and stiff with age, yellow from a lifetime of tobacco. Nicole remembered her own father's fingers had looked that way most of her life.

The old man reached out his hand again and grabbed one of hers and held it in a surprising, wiry grip.

"But you know what? These crooked hands worked a lifetime." He followed this with a liquid cough. "But it's my mind that worries me. It's fading. It's still full of memories and the knowing of all the things I've known but it's fading too fast. And I'm alone now. No one to tell these things to."

"But Mr. Harrison, what about your kids? I thought you had two grown children?" Nicole levered herself into the bedside chair still holding his hand.

The old man didn't answer. Instead he said, "They say alone is only a word but it's not. It's a place. It's the place we all end up."

He released her hand and sat back against the pillows to

look at her. "You have soft eyes. Blue eyes," he said, "Soft like the skies in France the day we marched through Paris. That was a day! A joyful day." His voice dropped to a rough whisper and his eyes shifted to the window of his small room where a crescent moon was beginning to show through the pane.

"I wish you could hear the shouts, feel the women's kisses. Couldn't understand a word they said but their joy made it all worthwhile. When we came home I went back to farming out in Saskatchewan. You ever been there?"

Nicole shook her head.

"The land was so wide and the skies so clear, the stars so sharp you could hear them singing. On a winter prairie night you could hear the sound of starlight."

"You can't hear starlight, Mr. Harrison."

"Well I sure did back then," he went on. "It tinkles like tiny bells."

He coughed and spat into a Kleenex. Nicole brought the small garbage from the floor for him to drop it into.

"And then the fire. I can still feel those blisters eating into the flesh of my hands that day when I was fightin' that fire, breathin' prairie smoke, skin smeared black, diggin' that trench, wide as the wheat stands. My wife and son throwing flour sacks soaked in the well over the farmhouse roof. Do you pray? I'll tell you we prayed that day! There's a whole lot of fires again these days and I sure know what that's like. I feel so sorry for all those folks losin' their homes."

He sighed and closed his eyes. He was silent for so long she thought he had fallen asleep. She got up to turn out the light but his eyes opened suddenly and he continued in a louder voice. "We prayed that day, girl. And we won...we won! That fire never got us. It got a lot of people, but not us." He coughed again.

"Can I get you a cup of tea, Mr. Harrison?" she asked.

"No, no please stay," he said. "Sit down. Just stay awhile. Look," he leaned over, fumbled in his bedside drawer and brought out a tattered billfold, so old it was impossible to tell what colour it might once have been. "Look...my wife. She was beautiful then. She faded, you know, like this picture, as the years went by. I carry her in my wallet here to keep her with me always. But I still see her, I do. Young and beautiful just like she was the day we danced our wedding waltz in the Old Swede's barn."

He wiped his face with the sleeve of his blue plaid pajamas then seemed to grow angry. She knew the pattern but she also knew this was one resident who did not have true violent fits. Some of them could be so filthy-mouthed and vicious she tried to avoid them when she could but Mr. Harrison was a romantic, a talker. He reminded her a little of her father although Dad's voice had always been gentle and slow like a summer wind, not the creaking of an old door like this old man.

It still made her sad to know her Father was never given the kind of care she was able to give to these people. He had died alone in a small apartment in Calgary after he and Nicole's Mother had divorced. In a way, everything she did to soothe her patients was a chance to make up for that lonely death.

She gave the photo back to him carefully.

"You couldn't know," he mumbled. "How could you? If you walk past her grave you might even think I'd forgotten too. I can't get away anymore, to take her fresh violets and brush the grass away. She did love violets. Little royal folk, she called them, dressed in their purple velvet best sitting on little green cushions."

He was quiet again, resting back against the pillows. Nicole closed the curtains and poured fresh water in his bedside jug.

"Say," he said, sitting up. "Would you take her the violets? I have them there on the window ledge in that little pot. I order them from the flower shop in the lobby except…well I don't know why I still do since I can't get there anymore. If you take them, she'll know who they're from. You don't need to say a word." His faded blue eyes were pleading and moist as they looked at her. She stared at him for a moment. Her Father's weathered, face peered out at her from this old man's eyes.

"Mr. Harrison," Nicole said. "You know what? I might be able to do better than that if you like. I could take you. I can sign you out for an afternoon and we can drive over to the cemetery. It's not that far. Then you can take the violets to her yourself. It'll have to be soon though because I will be off after next week." She indicated her extended belly.

"Ahhh children," he sighed. "We had children. For a while we were a family. Don't laugh if I tell you this but…they were the diamonds in my life, those kids. They and my lovely wife." He covered his eyes with one trembling hand. "And I lost them all. I don't even understand how it all happened. If you've got family, you hear me girl?" He dropped his hand and glared at Nicole. "You hold them tight they turn to smoke right there in your arms and then…"

Nicole came and sat back down on the side of the bed and touched his hand lightly.

"What happened to them?" she whispered. He seemed much thinner than he had even a few months ago when she had been able to wheel him outside in the summer sun. Dad had shriveled up like dried deer hide too. He had lost the fire in his soul and stopped eating. He gave up and wasted away, living only for the next cigarette and the occasional visit from her or, even more rarely, her siblings.

"Jim, my son, he went to jail," the old man continued. "He had a good heart, you understand, but somewhere...how can I tell it? The farm was dying, drying up, just blowing away in that hot wind. I would go out to stand on the porch at night and I could hear it groaning like it was just lying there moaning, cracking and dying. The corn and the wheat just turned to dust. My son was restless; wouldn't wait for the rain. He heard green valleys calling from out in BC and he took off. They say it wasn't as bad here in the Canadian prairie as down in the American Midwest but don't you kid yourself. It hit us hard too. The dust. I'll never forget the dust. We lived with the dust, we ate it, slept in it, watched it strip away everything we had. Oh it was real all right."

His voice began to fade as if the sadness of his story was taking his strength with it. Nicole waved through the door to another staff member passing down the hall who had glanced in to make sure there was no problem. She was off shift soon anyway. Mr. Harrison looked at up at the movement.

"Where was I?" he asked.

"You were saying about your son?" she prompted. She had heard parts of the story before but only in disjointed fragments. His thoughts seemed to be flowing in a linear pattern tonight which was unusual. He had been out in the garden this afternoon and maybe the clear summer air helped to clarify his thoughts. It always did that for her too.

"That's right. My boy, Jim. He was gone. All he took was a sack and that scrawny horse that died before he ever reached the coast. And I don't blame the boy for what he did. Would you?" he spoke the last words as a challenge but didn't give her time to respond.

"You don't know! You're so young. What do you know of life?" Nicole felt a rush of irritation at his words. Little did he know what it had cost her to even get this job; to survive on her salary and Matt's and now with a baby coming…

She held a glass of water to his lips. She needed to get him settled and clock out. He turned his head away and wouldn't drink.

"What do you know of watching your wife walk every day in that burning sun, ankle deep in God forsaken dust, walking down the lane, praying for a letter that never came. I'd see her slowly turn around and drag herself back to the empty house. A son in prison, a daughter… better to forget about her. She went off to make a better life for herself. And she did and I'm glad but after that she never did have the time of day for me."

Tears dribbled down his flannel cheeks and his nose began to run.

"Mr. Harrison, please. You shouldn't upset yourself like this." Nicole handed him another Kleenex but he ignored that too. Just let the wet glisten on his face.

"You know," he said, more softly now. "If I close my eyes I almost hear my daughter's voice in yours. Soft, like a spring wind when it flowed through the new corn. Your hair was soft then, soft and blond like the corn silk…like the fox-tails that grew by the pond. Remember? I would brush it on Sundays while your Mother slept. Remember? The touch of my hands?" He held his hands out in front of him. They shook with the effort.

"My hands worked then," he said, still gazing at his twisted, gnarled fingers. "They were good and strong. They could hold the plow while it chewed that good black dirt. But the land turned white, bleached, dead. I couldn't work it anymore, even with my two good hands. The air was full of dust the day you walked away. Remember?" He looked up at her, tears shimmering in the lower lids of his faded eyes. She opened her mouth to speak but he stopped her with an irritated wave of his hand.

"No, I know you're not her. Don't look so worried. Maybe you shouldn't have listened to all this. I'm ashamed. I don't like old people who cry and feel sorry for themselves."

Nicole touched his shoulder. She felt a mixture of annoyance with his tears but sadness too. She had never seen her father ever drop a tear although in so many other ways this man reminded her of him. Dad had been such a gentle soul yet he had the courage and strength to stand against the winds of life in the same way this man must once have done. She honored that strength. Some of the other staff didn't have any patience with him and would laugh at his ramblings but she could see the strength and courage still there behind the pale, flaccid cheeks, the yellowed fingers and wisps of white hair still gamely clinging to his spotted scalp.

"Can you see it?" he whispered. "Can you hear it? The prairie? It was like a breathing thing through every year of my life. The sky so huge it went on forever." She knew what he meant. She spent as much time as she could up in the mountains where she could see far into the eastern distance and imagine worlds beyond that.

"You need to get some sleep now, Mr. Harrison." She pulled the blankets up to his chin, reached over and shut off the bedside light. "But what about your wife," she asked quietly in the soft light from the doorway. "Did you want to go and see her tomorrow afternoon if I can arrange it?"

"When Maggie and I took over the farm," he ignored her question and whispered into the darkened room, "I planted a windbreak hedge all along the north side to keep the cold wind down. I planted canola the first year. We didn't call it that back then. Back then it was called rapeseed. It was something else in full bloom, let me tell you. Bright blazing yellow like there was a yellow light inside it. And standing there against the green of the pine windbreak all that yellow/green reminded me of something my Maggie used to make. Corn and string beans. She called it succotash. I laughed and made her tell me every time just to hear her say it." He chuckled at the memory but the chuckle brought a fit of coughing. He got his breath back and continued.

"I sold the farm. Had to. It wasn't the same without my Maggie standing on the porch where she always was, wiping her hands on her apron and squinting into the sun. She just wasn't there anymore."

"What happened?" Nicole asked.

"I lost her too," he said. "There's no one left now. No one who knew that world with me. I'll tell you a secret, young lady." He reached for her again. She had to resist the urge to pull away. "Old men do cry but we have damned good reason to. I don't mean to, you know, but there's a hell of an ache in my heart when I think of her. It's like a saw blade hiding in the hay; it takes me unawares sometimes. There's a whole lot of memories piled up in this old heart." He thumped his chest. "They bite into your gut. You grieve as much for the time that's gone as you do the people."

He took the tissue she offered this time and blew his nose loudly.

"So now I sit in that damned stupid chair and you girls wheel me to dinner like a kid in diapers and nobody will listen when I tell 'em I just don't want to be here anymore…"

"Mr. Harrison, you don't mean that. There are still things to live for. Out in the garden today, didn't you enjoy that beautiful summer sky, the gorgeous flowers, the songs of the robins? What about talking about old cars with my husband? You love that old Chevy of his and telling him all about what he should do to fix it up? You said you wanted to go for a ride in it. That's something to look forward to."

Nicole was beginning to get a bit worried about the direction of this conversation. She had seen this before and she understood how easy it was for their charges to lose hope and simply let themselves fade into oblivion. They say you can't die of a broken heart but she truly believed you could die of a heart that has lost hope.

"You're a dear sweet girl," he said. "Thank you for spending some time with me and for listening, but you need to go now. Get on with your work. You don't want to be spending all your time with me."

"It is time for lights out. Is there anything you need before I go?"

"Yes," he said softly. "There is something I really need you to do for me."

"Of course. What's that?" She smiled gently at him.

He stared at her. "Do you know your smile is like a closed book? When you finally open it, it lights up a world of wonders."

She laughed at that. She knew she was not inclined to smile or laugh easily and it made people think she was all seriousness all the time.

"Thank you," she said. "I'll take that as a compliment. Now what was it you needed me to do?"

"Would you take her the violets?" He gestured to the little pot of violets blooming on the dark window sill below the curtain edge. "Please?" he said.

Nicole felt tears prick at the edges of her own eyes.

"Of course, Mr. Harrison. Of course I will. If you don't feel up to going with me I'll take them tomorrow. I promise."

"Thank you," he mumbled as he closed his eyes. "Thank you. If you leave them with me they'll just wither and die. I'm clumsy with beautiful things."

Chapter 11
Silent Sky

(July)

There was no sound outside her window but she knew he was there. She could sense him, smell him.

It was every nightmare of invasion, rape and murder coming true. She stopped breathing; desperately trying to hear him over the roar of fear in her head. She was paralyzed. Her bladder threatened to let go in a burning flood.

Every warning from every well-meaning friend rang out in the darkness: "Sell the farm. Move to the city or at least into Cougar Lake. Get an apartment. Live with your son and daughter-in-law. You'll be murdered in your bed one night."

And now the shadow, silent, evil, stood outside the bedroom window. Could she hear him breathe? The shadow moved. Footsteps creaked down the stairs and out into the yard. She breathed thin, quiet wisps of dry air through her open mouth to hear better.

She lay for long dangerous moments before she even thought of the phone. Then she cautiously reached out to pick it up. The dial tone was terrifyingly loud and woke her to the empty sensation of the quiet house as she had come to know it since Martin died. All was silent. She tried to force her eyes to see in the absolute dark; tried to hear the soundless motion across the yard.

She stood up, twitched the curtains aside, and looked out

the window. She still held the phone to her ear. The farmyard stood empty in the moonlight.

The intruder was gone if there even had been one. Had she actually seen that shadow? Now she wasn't sure. It could have been a branch moving in the wind. No point phoning the Constable and getting him out of bed, especially if it turned out to be nothing.

Jean was shaking as she put on her robe and went to check the house. Moonlight filtered in through the windows and silvered each empty room. She checked the locks on all the doors and the latches on each window.

"I need a dog," she said to the empty house. "I definitely need a dog."

In the morning she realized that, of course, it was nothing but the imaginings and fears that had plagued her, keeping sleep from her night after night for the past year.

After the funeral she came back to the farmhouse: to days of sorting through Martin's things, to milking, gathering eggs, trips to town to deliver eggs and milk and get the few groceries she needed for herself.

Her son and his wife had helped as much as they could but Matt and Nicole were still recently married and getting their own feet on the ground. She wasn't about to lean on them. She knew better than to imagine 30 acres of canola and wheat could be planted, tended and harvested by one 48 year old woman on her own. Instead she leased most of the land and lived on the rent from that plus she still kept the milk cows, the chickens, and the vegetable garden. It turned out to be a good decision. She wouldn't have made it. The dry and silent sky was killing everyone this year; crops already withering in the fields. She refused to worry about what would happen to her if the tenants were wiped out and couldn't pay the rent.

"Don't borrow trouble," she told herself.

The nights, though, were more frightening than she had imagined when she first determined to stay on the land alone. She had to admit she stepped to the edge of failure more than once through that long, lonely winter. And then one spring morning she awoke to find she had slept the night through with none of the empty pain inside. The spring had been good. She thought she was settling in, adjusting.

Then... it all returned. Two weeks ago she started hearing noises, seeing ghosts.

It's just my fear I hear at night. There's no burglar. If there was, why has he done nothing, taken nothing? Perhaps I'll take a sleeping pill tonight.

In a baggy T-shirt, jeans and rubber boots, she headed through the summer dawn toward the barn. There was one small spot of mud in the dusty yard where she had thrown some slop water last night. And in the mud, a single, fresh footprint!

The sight of it sent a spear of electric adrenalin shock through her. A scream began in her throat. She stared as if the footprint might move of its own accord. It did nothing.

The town Constable, when he came, suggested a transient prowler, looking for easy pickings who must have come and gone.

"I wouldn't worry, Jean", he said. "He did no harm. Probably a transient on his way through to somewhere else."

"Roy, this is not the first time!" Her voice was pitched too high. "I don't think it will be the last."

He looked at her from behind trooper-style sunglasses. Roy was short and round as a bowling ball. She couldn't believe he took himself seriously enough to wear them.

"If you're going to be living out here alone I'd buy myself a dog. Or get a rifle." He smirked.

"I have a rifle, Roy. And I know how to use it." After he

left she went through her chores as usual but with an eye always over her shoulder. The relentless heat didn't help. July this year was deathly hot and still. There had been no rain since early June. By mid-afternoon she had to go inside to the relative cool of the house.

As twilight crawled in across the sky she got the Lee Enfield from the shed, cleaned it and propped it inside the bedroom door. She didn't load it but placed the clip on top of the dresser a step away.

That night she lay awake until well past 1:00. She was just drifting off to sleep when she heard him move across the porch outside. His tread was as sure and heavy as Martin's had been. A step that says 'I know this house and I'm not afraid'.

"You'd better be, you bastard," Jean whispered, fumbling in a panic for her glasses. "There's a frightened woman in this house with her finger on a gun; so frightened a rabbit twitching could set her off."

Her breathless whisper made no sound. Her ears were desperately tuned to the progress of footsteps across the yard. She loaded the clip awkwardly, cursing her precaution.

The footsteps moved off toward the barn; what did he want there? She crept toward the door then moved like a shadow out into the yard. Her real shadow stretched like a sliding serpent in the orange yard light. Her hands slid up the stock of the gun, oiling it with her sweat.

She visualized the prowler lying dead on the floor of the barn, blood flowing into the straw. She opened the barn door quietly, hands shaking. The cattle lifted their feed-dusted faces to stare at her. No sign, no sound. He had vanished in the night. Maybe he had doubled back to the house!

But the house, too, was silent as she crept from room to

room. It breathed its own night scents of only Jean and the faintest memories of Martin's earthy sweat.

Next time, I swear, I'll shoot right through the window the minute the shadow comes, before he has a chance to move away. Seems a fair bet there'll be a next time.

But next time strangely didn't seem to come. It had been six days without a sign. Jean had almost learned to sleep again, but the gun still stood beside her bed, loaded this time.

And then… he was there again. This time she got out of bed at the first whisper of sound. She waited silently. Patient as a hunter. She sighted down the barrel of the rifle and lined up the bead on the cross-brace of the window. She held her breath.

And then the shadow coughed. Just beyond the window he gently coughed. It took her by surprise. That tiny sound somehow made her phantom seem too real, too human. She lowered the rifle an inch.

Her father always coughed like that at night. She and her sisters would hear him on the far side of the wall and would know the world was safe as long as father lay there making those familiar sounds. When he died she felt alone in a silent house full of women and for a long time she couldn't sleep.

When she and Martin were first married she was delighted to find he had the same habit. He would cough to clear his throat from time to time while he slept. All the years they had been together she never once complained when a cough would wake her from a sound sleep. She never liked the silence of the night.

Jean's startled thoughts had given the enemy the edge. Now he was gone. She lay back on the bed, the gun across her chest. Based on the pattern of the previous nights she was fairly sure he wouldn't come back tonight.

I can't understand his purpose here. He never damages anything, or breaks into the house. Never seems to take a thing; just walks about the place. I half suspect it must be Martin's ghost.

But if a ghost, this one seemed harmless; unmotivated to any ill intent. If he was a transient he couldn't be very bright to stay around a small town where a strange face is commonly the centre of gossip.

It might be one of the boys from the neighboring farms or even my own tenant's boy. Whoever he is he must know me. I probably see him all the time in Cougar Lake. I may have stood beside him at the bank and never looked his way. I'll have to watch for clues.

Still, she called Constable Roy again and he came out and poked around.

"There's footprints alright but they could have been anybody."

"Anybody doesn't live here, Roy. I do. No one else."

"Well, one of the hired boys then? Your renters?"

"I haven't any hired help, you know that. And what would any of the Stewarts be doing hanging around here at 3 a.m.?"

"I'm just trying to be helpful, Jeanie. Since there's no damage and nothing taken there isn't any crime. So, at this point, there's nothing I can do."

"Can't you stake someone out here to watch? He'll be back."

"Can't do that," he says, staring out across the golden, late afternoon prairie. "Only got two men and one's away sick."

"Then you stay."

A slow, sly smile spread across his face. "Well, thanks," he said, "But my wife might not be very pleased."

"I mean the yard", she snapped.

His grin vanished. "Nope, can't be doin' that. You want somebody up here you'd best get your son to come out. Nothin' more I can do."

I suppose he thinks this is very funny. I've lived in this community all my life but suddenly I became "The Widow" and fair game when Martin died. And I am not going to bring Matt into this.

When he was gone she sat in silence watching the shadow of the barn lengthen and darkness seep into the yard. Strangely she felt relieved. In some odd way she was beginning to look forward to confronting her tormentor face to face alone; to try to find a reason for all the sleepless nights he'd put her through.

That night he didn't come. Jean waited, alert, but nothing happened. Finally she fell asleep on the couch with the rifle on the floor beside her.

In the morning she took her coffee to the porch and watched a cloud of Canada Geese sail high across her field, moving north. The geese passed minute after minute. Her blood soared with them in joy across the cloudless summer sky. She watched them stretch their glorious necks in regal determination. Their wild cry faded slowly back to her as the last few stragglers were silhouetted against the morning sun. She wanted to be free to fly like that. Maybe she didn't belong here after all. What on earth did she think she was doing keeping herself tied to this farm?

The sky was so hot and low she could barely breathe. Even the sun stood still in the silent sky. She took a deep breath. She'd slept late and needed to get on with chores. She turned to go inside the house and saw the egg basket beside the door.

That's odd. I always leave it on the nail in the hen house.

The basket was full. She stared down at the creamy curve of eggs piled high in the wicker shell.

I don't understand. Maybe Matt came by and gathered the eggs. Sometimes he did that when he was taking some out to the old woman and her grandson.

She peered out into the yard and up the road looking for any sign of the red Chevy. Nothing. She ran to the coop. The nests were empty; there was clean, fresh straw on every one and the floor had been swept.

I must have done it myself. I've simply forgotten. It's the stress of the situation, that's all. But why then leave the basket on the porch? I don't believe this. Am I starting to lose my mind?

"You'd better tell me who it was and why or I'll scream and stop your egg production for a week," she yelled at the hens. "Oh great, I've begun talking aloud. They say a person does that if they live alone too long."

There's no answer from the hens.

She trudged on through the blaze of the day; the sun so hot it bit exposed skin. She finished milking and started forking hay into feed bins. There was only enough hay for a month or so. In a good year the neighbors would have helped but they had their own problems with their crops dying in the sun; the soil cracking like over-baked potatoes.

That night the moon climbed silently in and out of thin wisps of cloud. Perhaps tomorrow it would rain. Around 2:00 the back porch door creaked open. Jean was instantly awake.

The main kitchen door is locked; I know; I checked it twice before bed.

There were no more sounds. She reached for the rifle but did not pick it up. The screen door clicked closed again and heavy footsteps crossed the porch and faded away. Her hands relaxed and she fell asleep once more.

The eggs were inside the back porch this time. Perhaps he feared a dog or raccoon might get them. The sky was hot again, no sign of the hoped for rain. She checked the cattle and found four bales of hay neatly stacked inside the barn.

She closed the door thoughtfully. A small red pick-up truck drove into the yard leaving a plume of dust for miles up the country road.

"Good morning, Aiko. Hi Louisa," she called. It was her turn to host Saturday morning breakfast for her nearest neighbours. "Coffee's on. C'mon in."

She poured coffee for them and then got to work making cinnamon French toast and bacon.

"I hear you've had a burglar out your way," Louisa said as soon as she sat down.

"He's gone," Jean told her, not quite sure why she lied. "A transient probably."

"Well, I still say you need a man around the place to keep riffraff away. I'll lend you mine." Louisa smiled but looked like she almost meant it.

"How is he doing? Any better?" Jean asked.

"No. He's so worried he can't sleep. If the bank takes the farm I don't know what we'll do. We should have got out years ago. I don't know why you stay. There's nothing to hold you here now."

"If you didn't want to move too far, what about High River?" asked Aiko. "My cousin and her family are there and they really like it."

Jean lifted her gaze from the curling bacon and looked out her kitchen window to where the yellow gold horizon gleamed with summer. One lone cow stood beside one lone pine, black shapes framed by dusty light. The old homestead cabin with its collapsed roof stood like a sentinel against a sky scrubbed of colour. The fields lay open like fluttering fans. A gentle winter had left the mice in plentiful supply and hawks were swooping low on silent wings. The hot air was filled to overflowing with the richness of grass and earth. She thought of an apartment in town or even up in Calgary. She thought of the noise. She thought of having to live with Matt and Nicole in their cramped mobile.

"My life is here. That's all I can say. And yours is too. Aiko, you and your husband came from Slocan in BC. Would you move back there alone if something were to happen?"

Aiko was quiet for a moment. "It was beautiful there but, no, I don't think so. It was so small and isolated I felt like a hibernating bear all winter."

"There, you see? No matter how bad it gets, our lives are here. And it'll be alright. You'll see. This is just a spell." Jean smiled and tried to repair the rip of sadness in the morning.

She fell asleep easily that night and hardly woke when he came in to leave the eggs. In the morning she stood on the porch to drink her coffee and watched him working in the field; planting late perhaps, but planting he is.

It was the first time she had actually seen him. He looked like any other man: jeans, work shirt with sleeves rolled up, John Deere cap pulled down to hide his face from the sun. The build and style of movement gave him away as being none other than the shadow she had seen so often pass her window late at night. She wanted to walk out then and speak to this man; to find out why. She didn't. She sensed it would be wrong somehow. He would fade into the heat waves like a mirage.

But she slept without the gun that night.

The tiny fingers of hay were fully two inches high and July was fading before he came to the house in daylight. He had managed to irrigate this one small field from the thin, dirty stream down in the gully. Each morning the eggs were in the porch and the cattle had been fed. Each night he checked the house and yard. Each day he worked the field awhile before he disappeared.

126

There must somewhere be a life for him that has nothing to do with caring for me and my farm.

And then one day he was there, standing in the yard, just inside the gate, his hat, in one big hand, hanging at his side. He stood as still as a deer caught in open meadow. His face was the round moon face of the quintessential farming man. Very plain wide features framed the saddest eyes of palest blue like the faded sky of summer. He looked like something washed too many times, once strong and crisp but faded now and gently soft with use.

Jean stood in the kitchen, hands in the sink, and stared at her ghost come to life. She opened her mouth to yell at him but the harsh and angry questions stayed inside. Instead she wiped her hands and gathered cold chicken, boiled eggs, bread and butter, cold beans and lemonade from the fridge. She laid this silently on the patio table. The man looked at her a moment, nodded, then walked over to the yard tap where he carefully washed his hands. He came to sit at the table and eat. Jean sat with him and studied him.

When he finished he bobbed his head embarrassedly in thanks. When he spoke his voice was thick and gentle with a heavy trace of an accent she couldn't place.

"Thank you," he said. "I hope I have been of help. I wished to repay you for using your cabin." He waved his hat up toward the old homestead. "You're staying there? But there's barely a roof, no water, no heat." She was stunned.

The tiniest smile quirked the corner of his lips. "Heat I don't need."

"Well, yes, of course. But…"

He bobbed his head again in thanks and walked away, leaving puffs of dust behind in the yellow light.

Jean cleared the lunch dishes, feeling completely

disoriented, and drove to town, watching all the while for signs of him along the road.

She checked in with the Constable first, being careful to keep her inquiries cryptic. No information there. The hotel clerk explained that, although she couldn't be sure, it might be the man they found sleeping in the hotel shed last month. He left peacefully when told to.

"Quiet man, was he?" she asked.

"Never a word to us. Maybe dumb and can't talk at all. Wouldn't that be something? Where did you see him? Constable might want to know. He's been asking us to keep an eye out for vagrant bums this past while."

"I've already seen the Constable," Jean hurried to reassure her, leaving her questions unanswered.

A vagrant bum? I don't think so. Anyone who works as hard for as little return hardly qualifies. Perhaps he's desperate, looking for work, and thinks this is one way to prove his worth. A pretty risky way. I'm not sure I should be letting him work the farm. Maybe I should go out tomorrow and run him off with the rifle.

She knew she wouldn't though. His pale summer eyes and gentle hands, his solid silence and hard work, told her everything she needed to know. He loved the land and knew it well. That was obvious. His work spoke for him, his eyes, his hands, his body spoke more eloquently than words.

When she woke one night to find the moonlight shining on the bedroom door as it slid open, she lay as quietly as he himself as he stood in the doorway. He waited for Jean to scream. And so did she. He must have seen the moonlight dance across her eyes and knew she was awake. Still she made no move. He stepped into the room and came toward the bed. The thought came to her that he could kill her now but that was ridiculous. He stood like a frightened deer in the moonlight.

She didn't move for fear of frightening him away. He would disappear as easily as a moonbeam.

Quietly she lifted the bed clothes and folded them back on the empty side of the bed.

He carefully removed his clothes, folded them and placed them on the chair beside the bed. His warmth was like a nest, a cave, a gentle soft enfolding. Jean rocked him like a baby and caressed him into sleep while outside the sky was filled with the rumble of the rain.

Chapter 12
New Life

(August)

Matt whistled as he scrubbed the Chevelle, sweating already in the hot August sun even though it was barely 8:00 am. He wiped his forehead with his sleeve and looked up. The old groundskeeper who worked for the mobile home park rolled up on his converted golf cart.

"Up and around a little early, aren't ya Matt?"

"Ah, you know. Thought I would get out here and clean this old baby up before it gets too hot." He waved the wet sponge in the direction of the Chev.

"'Bout time," cackled the groundskeeper "Them marshmallows must have baked on by now."

"Yeah. I'm having to scrape them off the windows with a blade."

"See you still haven't gotten around to getting the headlight replaced though. Surprised you've got away with that as long as you have and didn't get ticketed."

"The RCMP stopped me on the way to work a few times for that but I told them it just happened and I hadn't had a chance to get it done. Different cop each time though so there was no problem."

The groundskeeper gunned the motor of the golf cart that bristled with yard tools. He spat into the gravel and was just about to pull away then stopped, "So how is the new kid?

How're you liking bein' a Daddy?"

The now familiar stab of anxiety shot through Matt. "I'm learning, I guess," he said. He forced a grin and waved as the golf cart puttered away.

Nicole had given birth to their daughter in June and was off work on maternity leave from the senior's home. Matt was trying to adjust to a hugely different life and the reality had started to sink in. He twitched his fingers, drumming them on the roof of the rapidly drying car.

What the hell? I don't know what I'm doing. I am not ready to be somebody's Daddy. I wouldn't admit this to anyone but I'm scared shitless. Dad, I really, really wish you were still alive so I could talk to you. Why couldn't you have hung around for this?

He looked out across the foothills toward the Rockies in the distance. He could just make out the faded green of the pine forests in the morning heat waves.

I think Nikki is doing a helluva lot better at facing this than I am. How do women do that? Geez, us guys like to think we're tough but sometimes I don't think we've got a clue.

"Matt!" Nicole's voice came from inside. Matt jumped and the wet sponge went flying from his hand and hit the side of the trailer with a thud.

"Coming! I'm coming!" he raced into the house, not even bothering to take his shoes off. "Where are ya?" he yelled.

"Matt, stop yelling! I'm right here. You don't have to yell. In this tin can I can hear you whisper from one end of the house to the other." Nicole was leaning against the doorway to the bedroom. One arm cradled their little daughter dressed in just a diaper and a tiny T shirt. She had a point. Their home was a two bedroom mobile home with one bedroom at each end and a long hallway between that was broken up by an "L" shaped counter into a living room and kitchen area. There was a tiny bathroom tucked off the main bedroom and that was it.

"Are you okay, Babe?"

"We're fine. But I was really looking forward to a cup of coffee and a shower. I thought you would have put the pot on by now. And then I need you to watch her so I can have my shower."

"Sorry, Babe. Sorry." He grabbed the coffee pot, rinsed out yesterday's stale coffee and filled it with fresh water. "I've been out cleaning up the car. I want it looking good for when we take the baby to your grand-parents."

"The baby's not going to care how shiny your car is, Matt. And by the time we get to Calgary it'll be dirty again." She glared at him. Her wheat blond hair was tousled and much longer than she usually let it go. She blew it out of her eyes. "What the baby is going to care about is having to live in this sweat box." She walked past him into the living room and put the baby on a blanket on the floor.

Matt clicked the coffee on then squatted on the floor, tentatively rubbing the baby's back with the tips of his fingers. "Honey, I know this isn't the greatest. I was really hoping to have a better place by now but it's tough, you know. I'm workin' on it. I have an idea for down the road that might work but I don't want to get your hopes up. Just hang in there, okay?"

Nicole stared at him and then, suddenly, burst into tears. He was stunned. He loved his wife very much but damned if she wasn't impossible to live with right now. He knew she wasn't getting much sleep but then, neither was he. They traded off getting up with the baby as much as they could although it was Nicole who had to nurse her.

"Honey, don't," he said. He put his arms around her as she sobbed into his shirt.

Chapter 12

"Matt, I'm sorry. It's just…I don't know. I wasn't expecting it to be like this. I thought it would be all joy and light like the magazines make it sound." Then she said something that shocked him to the core. "Matt, I don't want this baby," she whispered. "I want to quit. It's ruining everything." She began to sob, swallowing huge gulps of air.

"Honey, yes you do! You do want this baby very much. And so do I." As he said these words he knew, with absolute conviction, that it was true. They had talked about nothing but the baby ever since they found out. They turned the front bedroom into a nursery and borrowed a crib from a neighbour whose son had outgrown it recently. The room was spotless and cheerful with its soft pastels and Winnie the Pooh bedding on the crib and matching curtains on the window. Glancing through the doorway now into the wonderful baby world they had created and knowing how much they had looked forward to having a family he understood that the anxiety they were both facing was only a fear of the new and unknown.

He stroked her cheek then stretched behind her for a tissue from the box on the counter.

"Babe, we both want this baby more than anything in the world. You're just scared right now. It's going to be all right. I know it. Let me get you some coffee. Then why don't we head down to the beach today. She'll love it. It'll be cooler there than here in this tin can, okay?"

She looked up at him and blew her nose. "You're right, Hon. I know you're right I just feel so overwhelmed. And I miss being at work. I really do. I miss being that take charge person who can take care of all my patients and be the strong one and….." she dissolved into fresh tears.

Matt pressed a cup of coffee into her hand. She accepted it gratefully then looked at him with a watery smile. She

133

reached out and touched the baby's soft hair. "I do love her. Very much. I do."

"We both do. And we'll learn to be a family together. You'll see."

"Matt, sometimes you surprise me," she sniffed. "That was the exact perfect thing to say at that moment. How do you do that?"

"Just 'cause I love you," he said as he kissed the top of her head.

Really? I said the right thing for a change instead of putting my foot in it? Nice going there, buddy.

He had always felt just a bit intimidated by his wife and it felt strange to be in a caregiving role. She was smarter than him, he had always admitted that. She was strong in a sharp-edged kind of way that left him breathless sometimes. He knew, if it wasn't for him, she could have left Cougar Lake after high school and done anything she wanted. Could have had a high powered career in Calgary if she wanted. He had always felt a little overwhelmed by the fact that she had actually chosen to stay here and marry him. He never quite trusted his good luck.

His pals, Kenny and Ray, had married girls who fit better into small town life than Nicole ever did. He felt a weird mix of pride and amazement when he saw the women together. She was like a prize race horse in a field of workhorses. He would die before he would ever say that to anyone but that's how he saw her.

"I'm going to pack us a couple of sandwiches and we'll head on down to the beach. What d'ya say?"

"I can't go to the beach like this," she snapped. The tears hadn't even dried on her cheeks before being replaced by a scowl. "I look like a deflated balloon with stretch marks."

"So you wanna stay in this hot tin can and sweat all day?"

"No," she sounded as sulky as a two-year old. "No. I want you to go out and buy an air conditioner."

❧

He spent the afternoon picking up a small air conditioner at Mike's Hardware store and installing it in the bedroom window. He made spaghetti for supper which Nicole barely touched. After supper Nicole closed the door to the bedroom to keep the cool air in and sat in their one rocking chair holding the baby and reading. With nothing better to do Matt decided to head out to his Mom's to see how she was doing.

"Honey," he called. "I'm going to go check on Mom. I'll tell her she's invited over for dinner with us next week for my birthday, okay?"

He drove out of town along the highway then up Range Road 40. Furrows deepened across the fields as the sun dropped below the edge of the earth. Cattle peppered the landscape while crops in every conceivable shade of green and gold formed a carpet of squares rolling toward the east. The rains at the end of July and early this month had rescued the crops.

Matt drove up the long dirt lane to the farmhouse where he had grown up. Tattered bits of gold-edged clouds drifted on the edges of the evening sky. He pulled into the yard and slammed the car door then stood and stretched his aching back as he looked out at the lavender light touching the farm and the soft hills in the background. He might have over done it a bit today washing the car then working on setting the footings for the new deck he planned to build off the back of the mobile, then installing that air conditioner for Nikki.

"Darling," his mother called from the porch. "C'mon up. I've got tea on if you'd like some. Or would you rather have a beer?"

"Tea's fine, Mom. How are you?" He climbed the porch and gave her a warm hug.

"I'm doing well, Sweetheart. Doing very well. Now sit and I'll get the tea."

He sat on one of the wicker chairs on the porch and watched the cattle gently rock toward the barn, leaving long-legged shadows against the grass. Across the valley a square of light blinked from another farm, barely visible in the evening light. He lifted his hand to shield his eyes from the dropping, amber sun. When he was little he used to try to catch the setting sun between his palms and hold it in his cupped hands. He shut one eye and tried it again. His fingers closed and the light slipped silently away.

He took a deep breath, inhaling the lost perfume, the rich, green smell of growing crops. It permeated his childhood. This is what he wanted for his kid. He wanted his son or daughter to grow up like he had. He knew Nicole hoped for a better life, a different life than what a small town had to offer. She dreamed of travel, adventure, maybe even a bit of the gleam of luxury. Not that she was driven by money. It wasn't that. It was a wish for new adventures, wider experiences. The same dreams used to impress him too.

But somehow having a child of his own new to the world, somehow those things just didn't seem so important to him now. He couldn't think of a better way to bring up a kid than the way he had grown up.

Shadows from the past flickered across his mind. Visions of himself as a barefoot child running across black fallow fields after Dad had plowed. Rescuing the nests of Ruffed Grouse or Killdeer that might have been disturbed by the plow. Catching frogs in the creek that ran behind the house. The warmth of a lemon sun streaming through his bedroom window in the mornings.

"Here we are," said Jean, as she placed the tea things and a plate of home-made ginger snaps on the patio table. "So, how are Nicole and the baby?"

"They're doing okay. Haven't been getting any sleep, you know. And she's got some wild mood swings going but I guess that's normal, huh?"

"Completely normal, Sweetheart. Just let it roll off your back. It will get worse actually, before it gets better but it's strictly temporary."

"So I hate to ask but how are you doin', Mom? You've been kind of acting weird the last few weeks, too. Are you all right?"

Jean looked startled. "I'm absolutely fine. You don't need to worry about me. I'm very much looking forward to playing the Grandmother role. Are you feeling a little worried about being a Daddy?" He noticed she had deftly steered the conversation away from herself.

"Yeah. Kind of." He brushed ginger snap crumbs from his shirt. "I think we're both a little scared, you know?"

"That's also perfectly normal. But, Matt, Sweetie, it will be the most magical experience of your life. Is there anything, anything at all that you and Nicole need?"

"Um, yeah. That's why I came to see you today. Something I want to talk to you about."

He tried to think of the best way to put this. He gulped his tea and watched the silhouettes of unbridled horses as they stood against the salmon sky, softly snorting.

"We need a house."

Jean swallowed and released her mug onto the table with an audible clunk. "Well," she said. "That was blunt."

Matt scuffed his hand through his hair and frowned. "I don't mean this place. This is your home. I'm not asking to move in with you."

Jean looked strangely at him for a moment but said nothing.

"I was thinking I could rebuild the old homestead place for us." He jerked his thumb toward the tumbled down log house that sat in charcoal shadow near the windbreak tree line.

"I could fix it up and…."

"No!" Jean looked at him with the weirdest expression. Shock and almost a look of guilt.

What the heck? The women in my life are behaving real strange these days. Worse than usual. I can't even try to figure them out.

Jean took a deep breath. "I'm sorry, Darling. I didn't mean to be so abrupt. It's just that it wouldn't be safe. That old place needs to be torn down at some point. It's not worth it."

She fingered her tea cup for a minute, turning it around and around as if inspecting it for flaws.

"Okay, Mom. I just thought since it's just sitting there rotting and empty."

Jean looked up at him at that. Her once hazel eyes were faded and the flesh was beginning to soften. She stared at him as if she was trying to figure something out.

"As a matter of fact, Matt, it's not exactly empty."

"What? What are you talking about?"

"I mean someone is staying there right now."

"Someone? Who someone? Why?"

"Please don't make a big thing of it, Sweetheart. It's just someone who's been helping me with the work on the farm for a few days."

Matt let out his breath in a whoosh. "Oh. You hired one of the guys from the Employment Centre. Well that's great. You need the help. But is it safe to have him staying here on the farm? Do you know anything about him?"

"I know enough. Now you need to stop worrying about me."

"Okay, but I don't like it. I'll take a wander over there when I leave and just have a talk with him. Just to make sure."

"Matt. You will do nothing of the sort. I am still perfectly capable of taking care of myself and making sensible decisions on my own."

Matt knew better than to argue with his mother when she took that tone. He stared at her for a moment. Yes, the steely determination was still there in the set of her mouth. He would talk to her about this again later but for now he knew he better let it rest.

Jean poured them both more tea. "So now that that's settled let's talk about a different solution to your house problem."

"Okay," said Matt. "So then I have another idea. Would you let me rent the quarter section on the south side of the windbreak? I could build a place there. It's just, we're going to need a bigger place and something better for our kid than living in a trailer park. I could do a lot of the work myself and Kenny and Ray would help. I'd have to get an electrician to do the...."

Jean interrupted his rambling. "Yes," she said, just as abruptly as she had said 'No' a moment earlier. "As a matter of fact I had already thought of that. But... wait here." She got up and went into the house letting the screen door bang behind her.

A moment later she was back smiling wickedly, one hand behind her back. "So I've decided I'm not going to rent that section to you after all."

Matt's heart slumped in disappointment.

She leaned over to plant a kiss on his cheek. "Happy Birthday, my darling boy." She handed him a large manila envelope. Inside it was the deed to the quarter section he had always dreamed of owning. It was shielded by the windbreak trees and had a fabulous view of the foothills and a sliver of a view of the lake. His name was on the deed.

"What?" He looked into the gentle face he loved so much and swallowed the threatening lump in his throat. "Thanks Mom. Thanks so much! You are going to make the best Grandma in the world. And if we're right here on the farm we can see you all the time. And you can see your granddaughter as much as you like."

She smiled. "I'm counting on it," she said.

Chapter 13
The Day Summer Died
(September)

A sudden blast of wind blew the chill rain through her clothes and deep beneath her illusion of summer. Janine unlocked the motel cabin door and stepped inside, letting her body adjust to the absence of battering rain.

"Why do I keep coming here?" She spoke in a soft tone, barely audible. It didn't matter. There was no one to hear her. The cabin felt cold and empty. She would need to start a fire to get the chill out.

She never slept well in strange beds but this morning she had awakened feeling unusually tired. She felt so terribly old lately. Every long, lonely year felt like another ache somewhere in her body. She didn't want to acknowledge the image of herself as an old woman; she avoided mirrors and kept active. Still she knew perfectly well that her short wiry hair was a dull grey and had been for a long time now. Sure she could dye it but what was the point? There was no one she needed to impress.

This afternoon her walk along the lakeshore trail had been an effort. It was tiring even to think coherently. Her thoughts glimmered and faded like fish behind glass.

She hung her wet coat over the back of a chair to dry, wiped her glasses with a tissue, and went to stand at the window, watching the silver rain.

"Rain!" she said aloud, her breath misting the window. "Why does it have to rain on my vacation? Nobody else comes back to the library after their vacation saying, 'It rained'. They come back with tans and tales of romance."

Janine sighed and bent down to light the fire the motel owner had reluctantly laid in the fireplace for her. He didn't see the point since it was only September but she was a regular guest who came every year so he wasn't about to argue.

"You're damned lucky," he had grumbled. "Most places these days don't have fireplaces anymore. Too risky."

"I know," she replied. "That's why my family and I have always come here. Thank you."

Janine always drove out from Vancouver at the end of summer and stayed in the small motel by the lake. Cougar Lake Motel had a strip of beach, a boat dock and several wooden armchairs nestled under a gnarled tree in the yard. Each year she noticed the motel getting more and more run down but she couldn't imagine going anywhere else. She walked by the lake with her binoculars, watching the birds, cataloguing any new ones she saw with a rush of pleasure.

In her memory, when she had come here with her parents every summer as a young child everything had been different. Her Grandparents lived here then, in one of the beautiful log homes looking out over the lake.

She was sure it had always been sunny and warm then. She and her father would spend hours splashing and swimming in the cool clear water while her mother slept on the beach. A smile of memory ruffled the fragile flannel of her cheeks. They ate strawberry ice cream cones on the hot afternoons. In the evenings they sat on her grandparent's front porch. On their last night Grandma and Grandpa would join them for dinner at the Copper Kettle as a special treat. Janine was delighted when she drove into town yesterday to find that the Copper Kettle was still there after all these years.

Finally the fire caught and orange flame began to lick at the wood. She stood and went back to the window.

Other bits of memories whispered in her mind but wouldn't be held to scrutiny. They burned away like wisps of clouds in the fire of a summer sun. That, however, was a blessing. She knew they would smother her if she tried to follow them.

Suddenly, outside the window, the mist shifted. A pale, watery light shone onto the dripping silverbush and cedar shrubs. Janine could just make out the line of pearl grey where the sky met the lake. And in that sudden light she thought she caught a glimpse of something that made her lurch forward against the cold glass. It looked like a child standing on the beach; just a small grey shadow in the swirling mist. The next moment the figure was running along the pebbly beach, long hair flying behind her like floating seaweed, and then she was gone.

Janine sighed, recognizing who it was. It was a familiar ghost. All her life she had been haunted by this ghost. The ghost was a young girl running frantically along this same shoreline. She could taste the panic in her mouth and feel the thudding of the girl's heart in her chest.

Her hair had been a soft, walnut brown then and the wind from the lake kept it constantly tangled. She hadn't cared. It seemed she had run forever on this lakeshore trying to escape into the magic bubble of time before that day.

The day when everything fell apart in her life. It happened the summer she was nine. That day her father had gone fishing alone in the cool of early morning, the time of day he always loved best. A wind came up suddenly, as winds do in southern Alberta. He was on his way back to the cabin, to Janine and her mother. Her mother had breakfast on the table and it was getting cold. She was worried, Janine could tell. Her mother stood at the window watching the water heave in the sudden chill autumn wind that came shuffling and whooshing up the valley from the east. They stood together not knowing that was the moment her father fell into the icy water. When the boat overturned on those very waves and slipped beneath the whirling surface; a crack in his skull where the keel of the boat struck. A trail of blood drifted into the water. He didn't have time to feel himself drown.

Later her mother said, through her own tears, "We should be grateful that it was so quick. He didn't suffer." But Janine wasn't grateful. Her Dad was a strong swimmer. If the boat hadn't hit him he would have been able to swim safely to shore. He would have come back for breakfast and the day at the beach and all the days to come. He would have been there at the dinner table with them every night and sat with her in front of the fire reading to her while Mother rattled dishes in the kitchen.

How could she be grateful when all that was gone? When all the years that followed were empty?

The more she thought about it the more her eyes stung with familiar tears. She almost believed if she concentrated hard enough on the rain washed windows the force of her will could turn time back. If she could do that she could change everything; keep him safe. She would cry and scream until he gave in and stayed with her and her mother safe in the motel cabin. She could always get her way with him if she truly needed to.

And she would know she had saved his life. He would never know, of course. Would never believe he had been in any danger. And everything from then on would be so different than the way it had all turned out. Her mother wouldn't have remarried and Janine wouldn't have spent the next ten years in fear of her new step-father.

"I'm not going to think about it anymore today," she said. She placed her palm gently against the glass. "Maybe tomorrow."

She put on the kettle in the tiny kitchen and made herself a cup of tea. The flames in the fireplace had dwindled to small tongues barely licking the coals so she knelt on the braided oval rug and wedged two more of the big cut logs onto the flames. For good measure she dumped the bucket of wood chips around the logs as well. That would keep it going for a while. The fireguard was bent and wouldn't stand properly so she left it lying useless beside the hearth. She settled down on the couch with a checkered quilt draped over her legs to enjoy her tea and watch the flames leap and dance.

She deliberately let her mind drift to happier memories from before that day. About the times they came here to Cougar Lake at Christmas to visit her Grandparents. They would go skating together, the three of them, on the cleared area of ice near the beach. When they were tired her father would brush off a log for them to sit on and her mother would bring out a thermos of hot chocolate. The chocolate had a faint coconut taste from the canned milk her mother used when she made it.

Their cheeks and toes stung with cold but the heat from their cups warmed their hands and their noses. The air was ice clear and the steam drifted into the cold afternoon, making everything shimmer with winter magic. It dampened the wool of her mittens, and her Dad's mustache would slowly develop a glimmering crust of frost.

Often her ankles hurt and her feet were cold becaue Dad's strong hands laced her skates a little too tight.

"Gotta keep those ankles supported, Pumpkin," he told her.

He would take off her skates and rub her stockinged feet between his huge warm hands until they tingled.

༄

Janine was older now than her parents had been then. She shivered. Why was she so cold? The fire was roaring and sparkling in the grate but she still felt a chill coming from the walls. One more log. Just a small one. She retreated quickly from the blaze as the new log caught and sent sparks flying. She snuggled back under the quilt with her tea.

"I need warmer memories on a melancholy day like this. Something sunny and bright," she said to the drab, empty room.

She thought of the summer they spent in Mexico, except she couldn't remember enough about that trip; just a swirl of colour and noise and smells. And there had been that dingy hotel where she lay for days sick to her stomach, wishing with all her heart just to be home in her own bed.

Better yet was the summer she and Dad had driven out from Vancouver together, just the two of them. Her mother had been working and couldn't get away. Janine got to sit up front with Dad instead of in the back seat. That was the time they stopped to pick peaches at a roadside farm. They ate their fill of fresh, sweet peaches and brought a huge box for Grandma and Grandpa. The peaches made her thirsty and Dad bought her a glass of milk at a café then snuck some of his coffee into it to warm it up.

"Don't you be telling your Mother about this. She'd say you were too young for coffee," he said with a wink.

Janine loved the sour warmth of it and the feeling of sharing a grown up thing with him. She smiled, thinking how her friends used to tease her because she still liked her coffee so milky.

She shifted and moved further back away from the heat of the fire. It was very warm now so she pushed the quilt down, just leaving it wrapped around her lower legs. She closed her eyes to shut out the familiar motel walls with their sprinkling of pastel landscapes.

She could see the peach trees by the side of the road whirling past the car. Sun danced through the orchards and gleamed on the hood of Dad's Studebaker. The dark maroon dashboard rose in front of her face and she had to peer upwards to see out of the windshield. Dad's thick fingers moved restlessly on the leather covered steering wheel. The wheel was so big she could have put her whole head through and watched the foot pedals from the other side. There were raised buttons on each side of the crossbar on the wheel and she knew what one of them did when you pressed it: the car honked really loud. Dad didn't use the horn much though. He just muttered softly under his breath a lot. She had been bored and curious one morning waiting for him to come out of the house so she pushed that button with all her might. The sound made her jump and Dad had come running. When he was sure she was not hurt his forehead rumpled into a fierce frown, grumpy as an old bear. She never did that again.

Sometimes he would whistle as he drove and then she knew he was in a good mood and he might let her talk him into things, like the day of the peaches. They hadn't been on the road very long when they passed an enormous, bright yellow highway sign proclaiming: "Peaches! Pick Your Own! Just 40 cents a basket!" Under the words was a glowing picture of a basket tumbling-full of fresh peaches.

"Oh Dad, look," she cried. "Can we, Dad? Please?"

"I don't think so, Sweetheart. Grandma and Grandpa are expecting us in Cougar Lake by supper time."

"But Dad, it wouldn't take long if we do it together. I'm a good worker. You always say so. We could pick a basketful really quick. We could take some to Grandma. She might even make a pie with them. Please?"

She smelled a hint of the pine-scented shaving lotion her father always used, mingled with the hot dust of the highway. She coughed.

Part of her nervously awaited his answer; part already knew exactly what he would say and everything that would happen. Janine relived this day so often in her memory she was afraid only of losing details over time.

"All right, Pumpkin. All right," her father laughed over at her. "I guess I could use a little break from driving anyway."

She bounced up and down on the seat and grinned at him. He pulled the big car off the road, swung it around and headed back to where they had seen the sign. While he was negotiating with the farmer, Janine ran to the nearest tree and looked up through the leaves with one eye closed against the golden glare of the sun. The heat of the sun was intense. The shimmering green leaves were almost transparent as the light illuminated them from behind and outlined the round shadows of the fruit. She could smell the ripe sweetness and feel the rough bark beneath her fingers.

"Honey, come on," her father called. "He gave us a section down this row to work. Now, we have to be careful," he continued as she came up to him and put her hand in his large, warm one. "I'll climb the ladder and hand them down. You put them in the basket, but gently so you don't bruise them, okay?"

"I'll be careful, Daddy," she said.

The farmer came up the row to meet them carrying a small

step ladder balanced on one shoulder and a basket in the other hand. He dropped them on the ground, gave her a wink, and went off to his own chores.

Dad dug the feet of the ladder into the moist soil. He wiggled it to make sure it was solid, then climbed to the top. Dad was a big man and a peach tree really didn't seem all that tall even to her but then she thought maybe all the good ones grew up at the top in the sunlight.

His hand started appearing through the green, leafy roof above her; each time holding a rosy fruit or sometimes two. The first peach she held against her cheek and rubbed the soft fur against her skin. Then she bit into its sweetness and let the sticky, golden juice run down from the corners of her mouth. She piled furry peaches carefully in the basket with one hand and ate them with the other.

They worked silently together as the sun burned down on her arms and shoulders. The peaches were heavy in the basket and in her stomach. Her father finally came down from the last tree and sighed; arching his back as he looked at the filled basket.

"Well done, Pumpkin," he said. "Let's go."

She lay back against the hot car seat waiting for him to pay the farmer. The sickly sweet odor of bruised fruit and hot leather in the still air made it hard to breathe. The heat was becoming oppressive and her mouth felt dry as sand paper.

She remembered sleeping through the rest of the trip to Cougar Lake with her head pillowed on Dad's rough thigh. Seat belts were a thing of the future. Every once in a while his hand would drop to her head and stroke her hair. It felt lovely.

She missed him so much. Even after all the intervening years the grief still curled through her like a whisper of smoke. It sedated all her muscles. Her eyes closed wearily.

The yard light had glared brightly when they rolled over the gravel driveway at Grandpa and Grandma's. Even against her closed eyelids it glowed.

"Daddy?" she said sleepily. "Carry me?"

His smile showed as a white flash under his moustache. He lifted her from the car and they jostled together up the steps to where Grandma was standing silhouetted in the doorway.

"You made it," she said. "I was worried. Is she all right?"

"Yes. She's fine, Mom. Just tired." Dad's voice rumbled through his chest just under her ear. "Too much sun and too many peaches, I think."

"You didn't buy the child peaches. How many did she eat?" She heard Grandma's voice but was too tired to open her eyes. She felt her father shrug.

"I'm not sure. We picked some for you too, Mom. It was Janine's idea."

Then she was being carried inside to bed. His arms rocked her like a tiny ship on a vast, swirling ocean. He would protect her from the swirling waves, she thought dreamily. And he would protect her from the lake when they went fishing together. Mother would stay and visit with Grandma while she and Dad went out on the boat to catch rainbow trout. The lake was so big it seemed like an ocean to her.

"No! Wait," she tried to cry out. "I don't want you to go!" She fought the heavy blanket of sleep. "Dad, don't ever go fishing again! Please."

She tried to tell him she was afraid of something but he just rocked her in the dark and said, "Shhhh, shhh, hush. Just go to sleep, Sweetheart."

Then it was the black water of the lake rocking her, swinging her weight with the ease of a floating feather. The clammy hands of the waves whipped in and out of the boat.

The icy water grabbed at her. She gasped and tried again to call for help. Where was Dad? He would save her.

There! His red plaid jacket flashed across her vision. He was here in the boat!

"Dad!" she cried. Why couldn't he see her?

Everything was confused in a rush of swirling mist. The memories were getting mixed up with nightmares. She hadn't been with him that day. She had been with her Mother at the motel. He was alone when it happened.

But she could see him. He was trying to reach an oar that was swinging wildly away on a crest of grey water.

"Dad! Swim! Don't stay with the boat. It will hurt you!" She tried to scream to him but she couldn't catch her breath.

The waves were filling her mouth and nose; choking her. She was sweating with fever even though the water was icy cold.

She had to get to him. She struggled against some heavy weight lying across her legs. She couldn't see what it was; couldn't see anything now through the thick air. Nothing except her Dad's frightened face. His cheeks above the wet, curled mustache were completely white. Her chest lurched with the horror of knowing that something could frighten this man. The man whose strong arms and rich laugh had carried her through the torment of childhood. He was afraid and helpless. How could that be?

She screamed again. Desperately she reached out to him just as he stretched across the water for the lost oar. The waves caught and tipped the boat. She saw him, in slow motion, as he twisted in the lurching boat. His arms lifted above his head, clawing at the air. The boat completed its roll and her father's body slid over the side and into the roiling waves. His head bobbed to the surface just in time to meet the keel as it dropped heavily from the crest of a wave.

"NO!" she screamed. "Oh no!" She tore the weight from her

legs and flung herself over the edge of the boat. The surface of the water met her with the force of a solid floor. Water seared her mouth and lungs like acid. She gasped for a last, stinging breath but her lungs resisted.

Suddenly she felt completely exhausted. She didn't need to breathe anymore. Her chest was a lump of iron. Her bones felt disconnected. Slowly she felt herself sinking. Flowing into the swirling charcoal expanse. Following him. She knew he was already dead but at least he wouldn't have to be alone. Not now.

⁊

Smoke billowed from the motel cabin window that finally broke with the climbing heat. Bright figures flashed through the rain, running for phones, running for buckets.

Call the volunteer fire department! Did anyone know if there was someone in there? No one could remember having seen the occupant but the motel office would know. Hurry!

The fire truck with two firefighters roared into the parking lot followed by a red Chev with two more men. Both vehicles screamed to a stop. All four men, rain-soaked jackets clinging to their shoulders, forced the door. They disappeared in the streaming smoke. A minute later, coughing, gasping, their eyes running with smoke-stung tears, they emerged.

One of them carried the lifeless body of a woman pressed tightly to his chest. Her silver hair suggested age but she seemed as weightless as a child in his arms.

Chapter 14
Memories Through A Prism

(October)

"Daniel!" Nicole threw one arm around her younger brother as he stood on the doorstep on a sparkling October morning. Golden leaves flooded the yard and drifted up onto the porch. Her other arm held the baby who stared at her uncle with startled green eyes.

"Woa!" Daniel said. "Hi there, Sis. And this must be the new member of the family. Way cuter than in the pictures."

"Come in. I've got the coffee on. I figured you would probably be on the early bus."

Daniel picked up his woven Mexican backpack that held his overnight things and his laptop case and joined Nicole in the baby cluttered living room. He looked around and his lips split into a wide grin.

"I never thought I'd live to see the day when my big sister lived in a Toys R Us showroom."

Nicole looked around the room. "I know. Matt can't quit ordering stuff from Amazon. It's like the baby is a new toy to him."

Daniel tossed his things onto the couch and followed his sister into the kitchen for coffee. He noticed the kitchen, too, was not the precise, pristine workspace his sister always used to insist on. "Baby changes your lifestyle a bit, does she?" he teased. "I see Matt's still driving the Chevelle. Shouldn't you be downgrading to a station wagon or something? You know, something family friendly?" He laughed as Nicole smacked him with a towel.

During the years after high school when he had been backpacking in the Yucatan, Mexico, Costa Rica and so many other places, his sister had been here in Cougar Lake making a life and a family

"Of course she does. Babies do that. You just wait. You'll see."

He snorted. "Not a chance. I have to finish school and make a name for myself before I even think about marriage and kids."

His travels had finally brought him home again to Canada and the amazing experiences had triggered the desire to go back to school to study journalism at SAIT. Calgary also had the benefit of putting him closer to Nicole and Matt and his new niece.

"How is school going?" Nicole expertly poured him 3/4 of a big mug of coffee with one hand and got the milk out of the fridge.

He topped up the cup with milk. "Hey, you even remember how I like my coffee. Thanks. So school's going well. First year Journalism was pretty boring but this year's more interesting. We get to do more creative stuff. Plus we have a freer hand to come up with our own projects. Like this research project I came here to do." He took a gulp of the milky coffee then wrapped his cold hands around the cup.

He watched Nicole put the baby into a colourful swing contraption and turn it on. It started moving gently back and forth and played a tinkly version of 'The Wheels On The Bus'.

"So I lined up the interview with Mr. Harrison for tomorrow," she told him. "I just hope he's having a good day when you get there. Sometimes he doesn't and he won't talk or he gets confused but some days he really rambles and you'll be able to get some great stories from him for your piece."

"Thanks Sis. I really appreciate you suggesting this. I didn't think there were any of the old guys left who served in WWI. How old is he anyway?"

"He's 102, believe it or not. And he didn't just serve in the war; he was a war hero and I'm pretty sure he's the last surviving vet from WWI in Alberta."

"Wow. Interviewing him for my research project is going to be fantastic."

"If he'll talk to you. I can't guarantee that."

"I know. You warned me. But I actually have a back-up plan, just in case." He grinned at her. She looked exhausted, he thought, and there was a strain around her eyes he had never noticed before. But her dark blond hair, so much like his own, was clean and brushed and she looked pretty in a tired sort of way. Whenever she glanced over at the baby a soft look of wonder came over her face for a moment before the strain came back.

"What's the back-up plan?" Nicole asked.

"Do you use Facebook much? I don't see you on there a lot."

"You've got to be kidding. I don't have time to go to the bathroom much less poke around on social media. Why?"

"Well, last month when you suggested Mike Harrison for my interview but you said he might be out of it that day, I put up a post on the Cougar Lake community bulletin board asking people to contact me if they had a story of historical significance. And someone did. She and her Dad used to come here every year from Vancouver so she'd be a great source to talk to about the gradual changes she would have seen happen to this town and the area over the decades. She's been coming since, I don't know, I think she said the early 50's. Something like that."

"That's a great idea. Well, let's get you settled in the guest room, also known as my study. Then we can take the baby in the stroller and do the tour of the town, see if anything is different since the last time you were home."

Main Street had not changed in the five years since he had been gone. The people were different but the old, false-fronted buildings and businesses looked the same. A few more coffee shops perhaps. The old sandstone building that housed the courthouse still stood in elegant splendor covered in a cloak of autumn red ivy.

Harvest Festival was in full swing in the Community Centre parking lot. They wandered through the throng of people and wove between stands piled high with vegetables. Huge bright pumpkins sat in a bin near the entrance. There were more handicraft stalls than he remembered but the smells were the same: ripe apples, earthy smells from the produce, clumps of sweet basil and lavender, steamy curry from the Thai food van, and the sugary aroma of fresh fruit pies wafting from the Copper Kettle stall. The woman selling the pies smiled at him and he couldn't help smiling back. She looked somewhat familiar so he glanced at her name tag. Lisa, it read. He couldn't place her.

They continued on past the school yard with the basketball hoops where he had spent so many summer afternoons. There was the Lux Theatre where he had sat with his friends in the balcony and watched movies while snickering at the kissing scenes and tossing popcorn onto the heads of annoyed patrons below. There was the Copper Kettle…Oh how he missed the greasy hamburgers and plates piled high with golden fries and the chocolate shakes. He'd have to stop in for a bite while he was here. Suddenly he realized where he had seen Lisa before. She had been one of the waitresses at the Copper Kettle for as long as he could remember. He was surprised she was still here, and obviously still working for the Kettle.

He wondered which of the guys he had known still lived here. He kept in touch with a few of them but it seemed like people from small towns drifted to cities and disappeared.

The people and the memories felt like they were layered in time from teen years back to childhood with the most intense at the forefront and quickly accessible and the rest fading into a murky depth. He was still young but some events were already in a mist of distance and others were painfully sharp. He reflected that his memory felt like looking into the past through a prism; not seeing the whole, only fragments.

The following morning after coffee accompanied by toasted scones from the bakery and fried eggs from Matt's Mom's chickens, he walked with Nicole to the senior's home and met the old man he was here to interview.

Mike Harrison was pretty cool even though he looked frighteningly like a skeleton with blue veined skin stretched too tightly over his bones. His hands were swollen and stained a weird yellow. Nicole said he had been a heavy smoker all his life just like their Dad had been. The fingers twitched and plucked at his clothes continually as they talked.

Mr. Harrison rambled wildly, mostly about his years on his farm. It was a little tricky to get him focused back on the war years each time he wandered away down a different path but eventually Daniel got enough material for what he felt would be a really great story. Especially the stuff about the Battle of the Marne. Dan had never heard of it before. Harrison said the Allied and German forces tried to outflank each other back and forth in a series of moves that ended up with the opposing forces facing each other along an uninterrupted line of trenches from Alsace to Belgium's coast.

How the old guy could remember all that and not remember what he had for breakfast was weird but in Psychology class at college there had been a section on memory. Apparently memory works almost in reverse so the earlier, more intense events stay in long term memory. Unconnected events, devoid of emotional impact, are stored in short term memory and quickly lost. Harrison's war years and the early years when his kids were young were obviously the most intense of his life.

"There's something else you should know, young man." Mike's voice was getting hoarse and his head drooped for a moment. He snorted and snapped his head back up. "We never knew when a German shell was gonna land in our laps. And every time when it didn't, you knew it landed in some other guy's lap. Maybe a friend of yours, a buddy in another trench. And every damn time you'd feel a rush of relief that you'd been spared for a few more minutes. Then you felt guilty as hell that you survived when somebody else didn't." He coughed again.

That hit Daniel in the gut. Mike drifted back to sleep for a moment which gave Dan time to swallow and remind himself they were talking about a war that had been over for more than 80 years. This was not about him. This was not about his life.

"Where were we?" Mike awoke and said with a rasp.

Daniel hesitated. Could he ask the question? Should he?

"I just wondered, Mr. Harrison. How did you ever learn to live with that guilt and all those awful memories? The guilt of living when someone you cared about died?"

"Ah ha well that's the million dollar question, ain't it. I'll tell you what, kid. Ya gotta learn to accept that there are some things in life that are random and we can't do anything to change them. It's nobody's fault. Stuff happens or it doesn't.

You got to accept life and the universe for what they are. All of us, every day. And stop thinking you're so special that you have any control over it all." Mike coughed heavily and wiped yellow phlegm from his lips.

"Okay. That'll have to be enough," Nicole came in rustling in her crisp blue scrubs. "Mr. Harrison, it's time to get you down to the dining room for some lunch."

"Sorry," said Daniel. "I didn't realize I'd kept you talking so long. Thanks a lot, Mr. Harrison. I really appreciate it."

The old man held out his hand. "You're welcome, young man," he croaked. Only then did Daniel realize he had probably let the old guy talk too long. He shook his hand and was surprised to find there was still a little strength in those swollen fingers.

"When I get the story written up I'm going to see if the Cougar Lake Post will run it. Would that be okay with you?"

"That's fine. Get me a copy though, would you?"

"Will do." Then he waved to Nicole. "See you back at your place, Sis."

❧

He stopped in at the Copper Kettle for a lunch: a burger, golden fries and a chocolate shake. God it tasted good!

He worked on the story that afternoon, spent a great evening with Matt and Nicole sitting in plastic lawn chairs outside their mobile. They drank beer and watched the evening sky transition from gold to lavender to charcoal. The baby slept in Nicole's lap as they talked.

In the morning he went down to the old motel by the lakeshore to see the woman who had contacted him. As he walked down 4th street toward the motel something looked very different, very wrong. The little motel office still stood against the backdrop of the pebbled beach and the sunlit water beyond. The strip of small cabins that used to stretch from the office in an L shape around the parking lot had an ugly brown gap at the end where the last cabin had always stood. Yellow police tape encircled it.

And the smell. His steps slowed. That smell. Smoke but not the clean burn of campfire smoke. This was charred ruins, burned plastic, drywall, carpet, clothing…the horrifying smell of a burned building.

"Jesus!" He stood frozen to the spot just outside the police tape.

"Hey, you okay?" a voice called from the doorway of the motel office.

He looked up, dizzy, disoriented.

"What happened?" he managed to say.

"Old lady burned down one of our cabins. We're not allowed to clean it up until the Fire Inspector's been out from Calgary. You must have read about it in the paper?"

He stood staring at the blackened couch, the piles of charred bits of wood that must have been the ceiling once. The ash covered metal table, twisted and warped from the heat. There was a gaping black doorway that would have led to a bedroom. He knew what a burned bed looked like. He didn't want to see it. His hands shook as they reached out to grasp the tape.

"Don't be goin' in there, buddy. You're not allowed."

His stomach clenched and his breath caught in his throat. It was no longer an old motel he was seeing. It was a memory.

"Was…was anyone hurt?" The scorched grass under his feet smelled of wet ashes.

The motel manager walked out into the sunlight and squinted at him. "You didn't hear? Yeah, the old lady died."

Oh God. He felt a wave of nausea flow up from deep in his belly. The man's voice faded to nothing. He turned, stumbling, and began to walk away blindly. The woman he had spoken to. It had to be. But it was another fire, another death, that swept into his mind. Waves of smoke blew across his memory. Their mother asleep in the upstairs room of the home he and Nicole shared with her after her divorce from their father. The house in flames when he got home from school. Nicole standing in the yard wrapped in the arms of a neighbour, tears streaming down her face, eyes wide with terror. In his mind the flames raged higher than the house had stood. The house had already become a shadow of itself, a memory of walls and windows, a ghostly roof shape inside the rolling tangerine flames. He watched the volunteer fire departments blast water into the gaping openings where windows used to be. He could still hear the hiss of the steam as it rose into the air. He could smell that pungent, wet, smoky wood.

He began running, gasping for breath. He felt the pebbles of the beach beneath his shoes. They said the smoke took her life long before she could have suffered any pain from the flames. He had tried to believe it. All these years he had tried to believe it. But the horror of their mother's death in that burning house had made it impossible for him to stay here in this town. The memories sliced into his heart at every whiff of smoke, every sight of the street sign leading down the road to where the house had stood.

Nicole stayed because by then she had met her future husband but Daniel refused. And that's why he hadn't been back since. He thought the memories were controllable and he could come back and do the interview, visit with his sister and her family. He had not counted on this.

The woman had a soft, tremulous voice when they had

spoken on the phone. A gentle, haunted soul. Why, why, why echoed in his head to the rhythm of his footfalls. Why did people die like that? And always alone?

He panted as he ran, then began to slow his steps. He swiped at the tears on his cheek. He stopped, bending forward, resting his hands on his knees and just breathed. The fresh wind off the lake brought oxygen back to his lungs.

Slowly he began to walk back to Nicole and Matt's, taking a roundabout route up along the railway line so as not to have to go past the motel. He was glad he was headed back to the city tomorrow. He would go now if he could but that would hurt his sister. He knew that. How could she live here with those memories trapped inside? He knew he couldn't.

The town was a close knit community where lives overlapped and sorrows and joys were shared but memories are your own and no two people's recollections are the same even if they share the same experience.

One of the reasons he chose Journalism was to write about the stories that build a community, the joy people share during their lives, the shared wisdom they can pass on to each other. But to also write about the deep sadness and loneliness that can exist even in a small town exemplified by these two lonely deaths. This old woman's and their mother's. He needed to make sense of these things that made no sense. He wanted to write true stories of things that happened but to shape the events around the lives of those who lived it. This is what fascinated him about Mike Harrison's interview. This was a life lived in the throws of history but still a single life with all the love and heartbreak a life can hold.

What was it the old man had said? 'Accept that there are things in life that are random and we can't do anything to change them.' Well that's true but how can you not wish you could go back and change things? The wish was palpable in his life every day. 'You got to accept life and the universe for what they are. All of us, every day. Stop thinking you're so special that you have any control over it.'

Talking with Mike, working on the story, helped him realize that trauma of all kinds lived in people's memories. Everybody had something; some shard that hurt to be touched. Maybe he could help by telling their stories. But most of all he wanted to write to try to shape the prism of the past into something that shone with colour and light and help him see his own life as a part of the whole.

The amber leaves rustled under his shoes as he walked up to Nicole's door.

"Daniel? Are you okay," his sister asked when she saw his ashen face. She stood in the kitchen doorway.

Without a word, he walked up to her, put his arms around her and laid his cheek on the top of her head. She smelled of baby barf and spaghetti sauce and it was wonderful!

"Oh Dan," she said, wrapping her arms around him tightly. "What happened? Something brought it all back, didn't it?"

"There was a recent…" he couldn't say the word. It felt like a hot coal in his mouth. "An incident at the motel. The woman I was supposed to talk to died a few days ago."

"I'm so sorry, Danny. I heard about the fire when it happened but I didn't realize… Oh God I'm sorry."

He took a deep breath. "I'll go back to the city in the morning," he whispered. "Sorry. I thought I could stay, but I can't." He pulled back a little to look into the familiar face so like their mother's.

"I understand," Nicole said softly.

Daniel took a deep breath. "But I'll send you the story on Mr. Harrison. I think it's shaping up to be the best thing I've done so far. Thanks for setting that up. He's a helluva guy."

Chapter 15
Storm On The Water

(November)

The cold rain stayed late into November bringing, not the bright snows of winter, but the wild grey torrents of a storm at sea. The streets became sluiceways; the soccer field a soggy marsh. Relentlessly it fell day after day, obliterating everything in an endless grey sheet. After five days of steady downpour the laneways in town and the dirt roads leading to dozens of out of town homes had all turned to a sea of mud. Cars slid along the soggy roads.

Mayor Susan Wilkes was at the old renovated wooden church that was now the town hall office. At the moment she was desperately trying to reach her husband at his law office on Main Street. The maintenance crew and emergency response team were waiting in the outer room for her instructions on priorities to deal with the storm damage. The office phone had been ringing all morning and some resident even had her cell number somehow. In the outer office, Dylan, her assistant, was desperately fielding calls.

Susan took a deep breath. She got up to go out and speak to the gathered group then glanced through the window and stopped. Up the road she could just make horses in their pasture stamping in the mud, heads down and resigned, ears drooping forward, tails clamped to their hindquarters. From outside her office she could hear the gurgle of flowing water as it made its way down the street in ever growing rivulets.

"Good lord, Barry. Get your damn horses under cover," she grumbled under her breath. She thought of calling the man but decided reaching her husband was more important.

"Pick up, dammit! Where are you?" She hung up and tried his cell phone again. He picked up just before it went to voice mail.

"Where are you?"

"I'm on my way to the school to pick up the kids," he said. "I heard about the evacuation and knew you'd have your hands full. Don't worry. I'm almost there."

"Oh thank goodness." The wave of relief was overwhelming. Thunder cracked outside her window and the room lit to white. "When you get home can you check on Dad too? He should be fine but you know how out of touch with reality he is now. He might be freaking out about the storm."

"I will. See you when you get home." He rang off and Susan sat for a moment breathing deeply. She was so glad he was here in town this week and not at his Calgary office. She took a last gulp of lukewarm coffee then went out to the meeting room to talk to the men and women gathered there. Until this morning the rain had not really posed a threat. Even now she thought she might be over-reacting but it was always wise to be ahead of the curve.

""Everyone! Can I have your attention? The elementary school basement is leaking and has several inches of water already. We're evacuating the children to the community hall as a precaution. I need a team to go over to the school, make sure everyone is out, and see what you can do about the flooding in the basement. Dylan, have you had any luck with the phone tree getting volunteers out to pack sand bags?"

"Yes," Dylan said. "There's a group down at the railyard now."

"Great." Susan turned to Duncan, the Police Chief. "Chief, I understand you also have reports of trees coming down across the walking path through the park? I assume the rain must be undermining the roots of the trees on that slope?"

"Yup. I've got a couple of volunteers coming into town with chainsaws to deal with that. Plus I've got all three of our officers out doing rounds to see if anyone needs help."

"Thanks Duncan."

"Susan? Have we heard any weather reports that this might let up anytime soon?" one man asked.

"It sounds like this is going to keep up for at least the next 24 hours," she said. "I think the rest of us should get on the phones and start calling some of the farms and houses along the river and down near the lake shore. The summer cabins we aren't worried about but there are people who live near the water and their livestock are down there too. Let's find out how they're doing and whether they need help."

Her father, Tom, had told her about the time the Glass River that flowed down from the foothills into the lake, had floated entire houses off their footings and sent them down stream, smashing them into the bridge. He had been working on the rail lines then and the mud slides had torn up entire sections of track.

Please don't let this be a storm like that. These people are struggling enough just to make ends meet. We don't need this too.

Her first call was to the volunteer fire Chief. She reached him on his cell at work at the Exshaw Cement plant. "Kenny, I'm glad I could reach you. Who have you got on call here in town and not up at the plant?"

Ken's voice cut in and out because of the weak signal in the mountains but she managed to get some of it. "Matt and I are here at the plant but.... (Static)...Ray Felden's on call... and maybe… (Static)…the truck… (static)…you … a key to the station?"

"I think you asked if I still have a key to the station?" She yelled into the phone not knowing why that would help. She knew this had to do with the very sketchy cell coverage in Exshaw where he worked, not with the volume of her voice. "I do, yes. I'll call Ray and see if he can round up some more of the volunteers. Is there any way you and Matt can take the afternoon off and come back? I have a feeling we're going to need all the help we can get."

"Probably not but …" The phone went silent. She quickly sent a text to Ray who was Deputy Fire Chief when Kenny was not available. 'Ray, we could use the truck and any men you can gather. Let me know.' She hit send.

Her assistant popped his head around the door to her office. "We've got a problem," he said. "The lake's rising, and fast. We haven't been able to reach some of the people up the valley, especially the ones alongside the river."

"Have we got anybody with a 4x4 we can send up there?"

A figure stepped into the front office, closing the door forcefully behind him to keep out the deluge. Water sluiced off his cowboy hat and puddled on the floor.

"Mayor Wilkes? I came down to see what I could do to help." He pulled off his hat to reveal short cropped grey hair over a strong but aging face. Too many years of alcohol abuse showed in the drooping eyes and jowls but his new life in the renovated mobile at the edge of town was starting to show a renewed strength in his sun darkened skin and clear eyes.

"Paul. My God you are just exactly what I need right now. How did you know? Living up there out of touch I thought we might have to come and rescue you."

"Well I've seen it before. Not maybe quite this bad but I've seen what water can do."

"You have a four wheel drive don't you? Could you please drive up Simon's Valley Road and see if anyone along there needs help? Apparently the river is rising and starting to wash away the banks. Some of those people have houses too close."

"Will do," Paul said. "I'll keep in touch. By the way, I stopped by the old lady's place near me and checked on her and her grandson. They should be okay. They've only got little Anderson Creek running past their place and it's far enough from the house."

"Thanks, Paul. That's great." Susan grabbed her rain coat. "Dylan? I'm going to drive over to the bridge and see what things look like. Call if anything changes." She headed out into the grey veil of rain. The parking lot ran with several inches of water. She sloshed through it to her car.

On Main Street she recognized Lisa Campbell and the other staff from the Copper Kettle hustling up and down the street, hoods up, wet hands helping each shopkeeper to roll up the soggy awnings in front of their businesses and bring in chairs and tables from the outdoor patios.

A red Chevrolet with a missing headlight pulled up beside her car. The window rolled down. "Mayor Susan," Nicole called to her.

Susan waved and rolled down her window too. She had to smile at the adorable baby strapped safely in the car seat in the back.

"Are you doing okay, Nikki? And the baby?"

"We're fine but I'm a little worried about Jean up there on the farm by herself. Matt's still at work so I'm going to drive up there and make sure she's okay. Is there anyone out that way you think I should check on?"

"No. They should be okay. They're high enough on the hillside for the most part. The only ones I might worry about would be the Mizukis: Aiko and her husband. They just moved here last year from the Slocan Valley in BC."

"Yes," Nicole said, raising her voice over the drumming of the rain on the car roof. "I've met Aiko. Their farm is pretty high on the slope though, isn't it?"

"Yes, but their paddock where they keep the horses is down on the other side of River Road from their farm and it's really near the water. Plus they have that huge stand of Birch trees above them and above that is that damned clear-cut section. If that slope destabilizes those trees could come down on them with no warning."

"Oh my God. I hadn't thought of that. I'll call her and see if they'll come up and stay with Jean and me at Jean's farm."

"Thanks Nicole. Shouldn't you be driving your jeep instead of this old girl?"

Nicole frowned. "I should and I would if Matt hadn't taken it to work?"

Susan left that alone. "If you reach Aiko tell her I'll be driving out that way so I'll check on them. Stay safe."

Nicole nodded and drove off. She was lost in the grey deluge in less than a minute. Susan's cell phone rang. The caller ID was blocked. "Hello?"

"Mayor Wilkes?" asked a trembling voice. "It's Lynn. Kenny's wife. Kenny's at work and I don't know who to call but my basement is starting to flood. It's already above the bottom step." The desperation in her voice was palpable.

"Okay, Lynn. Don't panic. We've got the police doing rounds to check on people. I'll have Dylan give them a call and send a car over to you. In the meantime, do you have a second floor you can go to? I can't remember?"

"No. It' just a small house."

"Okay. I'll send the guys as soon as I can. Listen, if it gets bad just get out. Come down to the Community Centre, okay?" She swiped the call off and dialed her home number. She didn't really expect her father to answer. In the last year he had lost most of his mobility due to arthritis which is why she and her husband had insisted he move in with them. She left a message for her father, Tom, hoping he would be able to hear it as the answering machine recorded it. She had the volume turned up on the machine for just that purpose.

The new arts and crafts gift store at the corner of Second St. had its door hanging wide open and the two friends who had started the store this past summer were wrestling with a huge tarp they were trying to drag inside. Susan pulled over.

"Do you need some help?"

Sheila and Janet stopped, wiped water from their faces and peered at her through the rain. "Mayor Wilkes. Hi. We borrowed this from next door. We need to cover all our stock. Our roof is leaking."

"Is it bad?"

Sheila glanced at her friend. "Super bad," she said. "It's pouring down the wall. We couldn't afford to have the place inspected before we moved in so we didn't even know." Sheila seemed close to tears.

Susan parked and got out of her car. She grabbed a corner of the heavy, slippery tarp. "Let's get this inside."

They dragged the tarp in through the door then each took a corner and pulled the heavy tarp up and over as much of the stock as they could cover. Susan rubbed her aching shoulders and looked up at the rivulets of water pouring down the front wall.

"You weren't kidding. Do you need some buckets or anything to catch all that?"

Sheila wiped her hair and face with a damp towel as she said, "I called my boyfriend and he's coming down from Calgary on the afternoon bus. He says he can patch it for us. Apparently there's this tar fiberglass quick patch stuff that you can put on even in the wet. He's bringing a couple of cans of it down with him."

"Did you check with Joe at the Hardware store?"

"Neil, my boyfriend, called him to see if he had any. He did but he's out. Apparently Joe's getting swamped with calls for all sorts of things like that."

"Okay. I'll pop in and see how he's doing. Well good luck girls. If you need anything give me a call." Her phone rang with a text message. It was from Ray. 'Got your message. On my way to pick up fire truck.' She sighed with relief.

The coffee shops and the Copper Kettle were doing a roaring business with people crowding in to get out of the incessant rain. Their windows were steamed up so completely that all Susan could see from the outside was a smear of colour and movement behind a screen of condensed droplets. Water swirled around the drains on the street corners. It was foaming up, not flowing down.

"Great. Now the sewers are going to back up."

She pushed her way past a crowd at the cash in the hardware store. People were stocking up on buckets, candles, blankets, matches and all manner of other emergency supplies.

"Joe!" she called over the heads of the shoppers. Joe's face appeared at the top of a ladder. He looked frazzled. "Just wanted to see if there is anything you need."

He swept a lock of grizzled grey hair from his flushed face. "Not unless your influence extends to the gods."

She laughed. "If you have any extra buckets I think the girls in the craft store could sure use them."

"Yup. No problem. I'll send one of my boys over when they get here from the school. They both stayed to help with the leak in the basement."

"Thanks, Joe. Good luck".

As she continued down toward the lake front to assess the water level she saw occupants of many of the houses peering around half open doors or through fogged windows, obviously trying to work out how seriously to take the situation. As she approached the old motel with its burned out end unit still black from the recent fire she saw the manager dashing through the rain knocking on doors. He waved to her as she slowed but didn't seem worried.

She drove onto the bridge and pulled over to the rail, idling the engine and flicking on her hazard lights. The bridge spanned the Glass River just up from the point where it flowed into Cougar Lake. She wiped the condensation from her passenger side window, peered up river. She had never seen the Glass flow like this before. It frothed white with foam but the water beneath looked dark mocha from all the mud being sucked in off the banks. There didn't appear to be more than a few feet between the roaring swirls of foam and the bottom of the bridge.

She grabbed her phone and sent a text to the RCMP detachment. 'Glass River possibly encroaching on bridge. Can you send someone to blockade the bridge and reroute traffic?' Worried now she kept on going, planning to just go up as far as the gas station at the corner of River Road and the highway to check conditions. She would turn there and come back into town on the highway to avoid the bridge.

The road was slick with toffee coloured mud in some places

and silver with several inches of water in others. Suddenly a mauve and blue shape emerged from the mist waving its arms. She braked and slid but managed to stay on the road.

The rain pelted into her car as she opened the door.

"Aiko, what's wrong?"

"Thank goodness you've come. Our horses…we can't get them out of the mud. My husband's down there but the horses won't move." She pointed a trembling finger down toward the fenced paddock. Two horses were at the bottom of the paddock which backed onto the lake shore. The ground, soft and spongy at the best of times, was a slick of soupy mud. The horses stood trembling. The mud was up over their hocks. Their eyes rolled in panic as they kept trying to lift one leg then another out of the sucking mud. Aiko's husband was securing a halter to the second horse, the first was already wearing one.

Susan pulled up her hood over soaking wet hair and they ran together down to horses.

"What can I do to help?" she yelled over the drumming of the rain.

"Can you grab the halter and try to get her to move while I finish this one?" He pointed to the haltered mare.

Susan pulled at the halter but the horse pulled back in the opposite direction in a panic. She then tried placing herself against the horses flank to push to the side just to get the legs to pull free from the mud. The mare lifted her head and whinnied but her legs stayed firmly encased in mud. Susan could feel the mud sucking at her boots as she moved.

"Aiko, can you pull while I try to force her from behind?" she called. Aiko had her blue and purple jacket hiked up over her head.

Aiko ran to the horse's head. Susan tried slapping the

horse's flank and yelling but to no effect other than the agitated flicking of the mare's ears.

Hiroto, Aiko's husband, meanwhile had the halter secured to the other mare and was tugging as ineffectually. "We can't leave them! We can't let them drown!" His eyes were almost as panicked as the horses' when he looked at her over the mane.

"We're not going to leave them. I'm going to call for help."

The water had risen even since she had arrived, creeping upward across the grass and creating a ruffled grey surface that erased the edge of the lake and made the paddock one vast pool. The rain roared in her ears and made it impossible to hear anything. The wind had picked up and was whipping the trees like crazy marionettes. What little she could see of the lake itself was a mad whirl of grey and white, endlessly moving. By this time all three of them were covered in splattered mud.

What do I do? I can't let these people risk their own lives for their horses. But how can we leave the horses to die like this?

"I have to go back to my car to make the call," she yelled and pointed to be sure she was understood. "Keep trying."

Back at the car she managed to reach Ray in the firetruck but he and his team were a long way off on the other side of town helping Kenny's frightened wife. "We'll get there as soon as we can but it'll be a while," Ray told her. "I'll put out the word and see if we can get some volunteers to get out that way."

As she ended the call headlights bounced down the road reflecting off the almost constant tumble of rain. She flashed her lights and honked the horn. The other vehicle slowed then pulled over to the side of the road. She ran over to the side of the 4x4. Paul stuck his grizzled head out the window.

"Paul. So glad to see you. Can you help?" She pointed to where the Mizukis were still struggling with the suicidal horses.

Paul calmly surveyed the scene then got out, not bothering

to zip his jacket or cover his head. He went around to the back of his truck and hefted some wide lumber and a tarp from the back. He handed her a long coil of rope and signaled for her to follow.

Aiko by now had given up trying to pull the horse and was crying and twisting her hands together in distress.

"We probably shouldn't pull on the halters anymore," Paul said to Hiroto. "If they fall they're going to break their necks. Have you got any strapping or even thick rope we could use for the hind quarters?"

Hiroto nodded and turned to slog back to his barn. The barn was only about 50 yards further up the hill but it appeared to be still on solid ground.

Meanwhile Paul carefully placed the lumber in front of the first horse so as not to startle her any further. By this time both horse were whinnying and snorting, their chests heaving.

"We're going to build a ramp," he said. "Give me a hand here." Between the three of them they managed to set the lumber into the mud as tightly as possible, edge to edge, in front of the horse, pressing each board into the muck until it held position. He wrapped the tarp over the lumber so that the surface would look solid to the horse. Hiroto returned with several thick straps that they were able to hook under the horse's chest.

With two of them pulling and two shoving the horse's hind quarters, her flanks shivering with effort, they managed to get the frightened animal to lift a foot and step up onto the makeshift ramp. When she felt the solid surface under her foreleg the mare lunged. There were awful sucking sounds as her remaining three legs came free and she flung herself up the rest of the way onto the little bridge, nearly bowling Paul over as he pulled on her lead. Aiko's husband had been pushing against the flank and lost his balance when she moved so suddenly. He landed fully on his back in the mud. Susan reached down to pull him up. He scrambled up, nodded to her and wiped his face so he could see.

A horn blared, startling them all. The horse twitched but did not move from her perch on the ramp. A massive pick up came through the curtain of rain pulling a miracle. A horse trailer! Susan recognized it as the one Jean and Martin owned when Martin was still alive. She was surprised Jean still had it. She didn't recognize the pick-up. Two solid middle aged men were seated in the cab with Jean wedged between them. She vaguely recognized one of them from the Saturday farmer's markets but didn't know the other man at all.

The four bedraggled rescuers watched in amazement as the truck drove straight off the road and onto the pasture which now looked more like a flowing river. Its oversized wheels almost disappeared under the water but still it came. The driver carefully turned the truck and backed it up to Paul's makeshift bridge.

"We heard you need a little help here," one man said. The two men released the rear ramp and lowered it slowly to the edge of the tarp covered boards. One man grabbed the bridle and pulled. The mare seemed to sigh with relief at the familiar sight of a ramp leading up to warm dry stalls and she bunched her hind legs and lunged up into the truck.

Paul immediately began rebuilding the little bridge in front of the second horse. The Mizukis and the two women stood back and watched.

"How did you know?" Susan asked Jean.

"Ray called me after you told him the situation. He remembered Martin's old horse trailer and thought it might be useful."

"Understatement of the year," replied Susan. "I didn't even know you still had it. "

"I just never got around to selling it. But you know something?" She turned to speak to the Mizukis. "I would like you to have the horse trailer when all this is done. I have no use for it." She waved away their thanks. "And you and your husband should come up to my farm and we'll get the horses settled in my old barn then I'll put on the tea. What do you say?"

Wordlessly Aiko threw her arms around Jean.

"It looks like you've got this under control," Susan said. "I've got to get going but you'll be all right at Jean's. Sorry to leave you. And thanks again, Jean. For everything."

"You're welcome. Tell anybody who needs to come to higher ground that they're welcome up at the farm too."

"All right. Will do."

As she drove away Susan experienced a wave of warmth and gratitude for the people she had grown up alongside in this gentle town. People who never let a human or an animal struggle alone. Those who pitched in with whatever skills they had to help someone else.

Her cell phone rang. "Susan, when you get back to town c'mon up to the community centre," her assistant said.

"Why?"

"Just come."

The Community Centre had been built at the top end of Cedar St. with a view out over the main residential area of town. Beside the building, the gravel parking lot was now a chewed up mess but it was full of vehicles, some even parked over the line onto the soccer field.

"What on earth?" Susan covered her head and ran for the door. Inside she was met by the merry din of voices and the smells of hot coffee and wet wool. Piles of boots crowded the hallway. In the main hall people milled about talking and laughing, most holding steaming cups in one hand and little cardboard plates of sandwiches in the other. A pile of dry towels, all colours and sizes, stood on a table beside the door. A bin overflowing with wet towels stood beside it.

Dylan ran over to her. "Mayor, come on in and join the rain party." He handed Susan a towel.

"How did this happen?" Susan asked as she toweled off the rain and the mud.

"Nicole arranged it. She figured we all needed a safe place to be and what better place is there?"

"But the drinks? And the food? And these?" She held indicated the towel she was now using to dry her hair.

"The Copper Kettle provided the coffee, tea and hot chocolate. The supermarket supplied sandwich fixings. And nearly everybody who showed up brought towels."

The Police Chief materialized at her elbow and handed her a steaming mug of hot chocolate, complete with a little white cap of whipped cream.

"Come sit down, Susan," he said. "You look drained."

"Thanks Duncan," she sighed as she sat in one of the old vinyl chairs. "Did all the kids from the school get here okay?" she asked. ""And the parents know where they are?"

"Yup. They're all back there. Even your two. You can let go the reins a bit now." He grinned at her.

In the back play room, just visible through the open door, Susan could see the kids playing board games around small folding tables. Her daughters were on the floor helping to build something with Lego.

Oh thank you, Universe!

"Have you seen my husband? I thought he was taking our kids home."

"No, I haven't," Duncan said. "I assumed he was still up in Calgary."

Dylan broke in, "Your husband brought the kids here instead when he heard. Then he went back to your place to bring your Dad here."

Susan's heart twitched like the flanks of the mare. "Dad can't get around!"

Dylan looked worried. "But your husband said there was a wheelchair he could use."

"Oh. Yes, I forgot. We don't use it much. Dad doesn't like it."

"Mayor Susan!" a voice called. She turned to see Nicole coming toward her with baby on her hip. "You made it. Is everyone okay?"

"I think so. How did you make this happen?"

"Just sent an urgent bulletin out on Facebook and people told other people, you know how that works."

"Well I didn't," said Susan. "But I do now. Thank you. This is perfect."

Familiar faces and a few unfamiliar ones shimmered in the room. Someone had set up a boom box and was streaming country music that lifted over the burble of voices. Through the blur of colour and movement she saw, to her relief, her husband rolling the wheelchair up the ramp they had installed last year with a grant from the Province. Her father and husband were safe.

She had just begun to make her way to them when a siren shrilled and an emergency vehicle approached the building. Susan ran to the door, braced for more bad news. The town fire truck came roaring up and disgorged more soggy evacuees; more people than she thought the fire truck could hold actually. She was pleased to see Lynn was among them.

"Come and get something to eat," her assistant said to her. "You look exhausted."

"I will but let me check on my kids first. By the way, Dylan, did you happen to notice if Barry got his horses in out of the pasture? You know the ones we can see from the town hall?"

"Yeah he did but not before that guy went over and gave him a talking to. The guy from the old mobile up the mountain."

"You mean Paul? He sure turned out to be a guardian angel today. Along with so many, many others."

She stood in the doorway to the play room and smiled. Her two little girls were playing happily and barely looked up to wave to her.

This is why we left Calgary and moved back here to live. At times like this I'm not sure why we ever left. It's a place where an entire town full of such diverse personalities can come together to take care of each other like this. This is why we live in Cougar Lake.

Chapter 16
The Last Christmas

(December)

The Christmas lights along Main Street created a rainbow glow through the bedroom window of a tidy two story home near the intersection with Cedar Drive. A string of red and gold lights outlined the window itself and created bright globes of colour on the wall above the bed.

Tom Wilkes rose slowly, with a grunt, from his chair. He stood at the window, leaning against the ledge, and watched the town fire truck move slowly up the street as the volunteers strung the lights up one length of the street then down the other. After a while the activity drifted out of his range of vision. All that was left was the silent snow falling. In the quiet he could hear his grandchildren's voices downstairs.

His own voice, when he spoke, was cracked and rough as sand. His breath misted the window. The silver light of evening was already busy turning objects from pearl grey to black while the snow traced the outlines of the trees in white.

"Christmas again. I'm getting old, Eliza. I am. Don't tell me I'm not. Mike Harrison's the only one I know who's older but look at him. They've got him in that old folks home where you can't do a doggone thing but eat and sleep. I still go see him every Thursday but Geezuz he looks old. The girls at the home treat him okay. I'm not sayin' they don't but I don't wanna end up there. Okay?"

He turned and shuffled through the rainbow coloured light to the washroom. He peed without shutting the door, then clumped back to the window.

"My chest hurts tonight," he sighed. "That's just because I let myself get upset, that's all. Couldn't help it. Little Jenny insisted on hearing the story about the burro again and wouldn't have it from anyone else. That was always our kids favorite Christmas story too, remember?"

"I didn't mean to spoil things for everybody tonight, Liza. You know I didn't. But the thing of it is I just couldn't see the words anymore. Not that I really needed to; know the story by heart. I just couldn't get my throat cleared to keep on. And then Jenny sitting on the carpet by my chair starin' at me, and all of them so worried and trying to hustle me up here to bed! Damn it, Liza, they don't understand. How can they? Do they all expect I should sit around and wait to die? I figure to see at least a few more Christmases come and go and have a good time doing it! Damn nonsense!"

There was a knock on the door.

"Dad? Can I come in?"

He turned and coughed, bending forward with a gnarled hand against his chest.

The door opened and his daughter, Susan came in. "I've brought you some hot chocolate. Are you okay, Dad?"

The old man waved a hand in her direction while he continued to cough. "Fine, I'm fine," he croaked. He sat down heavily in the armchair and indicated the table beside it. Susan carefully deposited the cup of hot chocolate on a coaster and slid it closer to him.

"I'm worried about you, Dad. We all are."

"Oh I'm sure that fine lawyer fella you married is really concerned about me. Did you send you up here?"

"No, Dad. Of course not. And yes, he is worried."

"Hmph. Probably about liability if I die in his fancy house."

"Dad! Why do you say things like that? I don't understand why you dislike him so much. He's never done anything to you."

"Sweetie, I'm sorry. It's just that he never seems to be here for you like he should. I am so damn proud of you being a fine Mayor to this town and he doesn't seem to notice. He's always busy working. It makes me sad, that's all. If your Mother were still alive, bless her soul, she'd give him a talking to."

"I'm fine, Dad. He's a little distant but he's a good father to the kids. And last month with the flood he came through for me then. He got the kids home safely and managed to get you into a wheelchair. How he did that, I'll never know. It's just, well, you know. It's just that with his legal firm they expect him to be at the Calgary office most of the time then he has his own office to run here. It's a long commute to Calgary so he's only home on weekends. But his income makes it possible for me to serve the community a Mayor in a job that can't pay much. You know all that."

"Why did you two move back here to Cougar Lake in the first place?"

"Dad, you know why."

"Because of me, you mean."

"Well, because we wanted to be near you. That was part of it. And because I wanted to raise Jenny and Kayla out here in Cougar Lake where I grew up. I love it out here. The city is no place for little girls to grow up."

"Well I have to agree with you there. If I could still drive it wouldn't be so bad. Do you know whatever happened to that old red Chev I used to have? The one I was going to restore? I sold it to some kid here in town. Is it still around?"

Susan nodded. "Matt and Nicole. Matt still drives it, believe it or not. A little worse for wear but it's still on the road."

"Good," he sighed. "The old beauty's doin' better than me then. Good to know she's not on the scrapheap like I am."

"Now Dad…"

He patted her hand. "Honey, you know what that doctor said just as well as I do. But at least if this is my last Christmas, at least I get to spend it with my family."

Susan's eyes filled with tears. She opened her mouth to speak.

"No, no. I'm fine," he said, waving away her distress. "You go on down to your family and finish your Christmas party. I'll just have my drink and go to bed. Off you go now."

"Alright, if you're sure."

The door closed quietly and the silence settled around him like snow. The sweet drink brought back winter nights and skating parties and flashes of evenings spent by a thousand campfires.

"You know, Liza?" he said. "Reading that story tonight with our granddaughter's head on my knee. It felt like the old days. In my mind's eye I could see our old house. The spruce tree outside the front window all covered in snow. Coloured streaks of light from our Christmas lights shining out into the dark yard. Inside I knew the air would be full of the smells of roast turkey, mincemeat pie, stuffing and gravy. There'd be candles on the table and red felt stockings hanging from the mantle. And children's voices. Our children."

The old man listened to the sounds of the present drifting up, in bits of high pitched child sounds, from the living room below. His two daughters traded him back and forth on Christmas and other holidays like a precious toy. One in Calgary, one here.

"Mike Harrison complains to anybody who'll listen, or to the air if no one will, about how neglected he is by both his kids. Doesn't even know where they are now. But our girls, Liza; we have mighty good-hearted girls. And they seem to like to have me. I need to feel I still belong somewhere, you know, not just taking up space. I hate it though. Hate being so useless. Being a burden to them, whether they admit it or not. I hate this old, useless body!"

His fist thumped against the chair arm. It was a fist thickened with a lifetime of work at the rail yards. A hand, stiffened and blue-veined but ready still to obey each determined order of an old man.

"Eliza, you know what I want more'n anything? To do it all again. To work. To see the girls running and splashing down at the beach in the sunshine. To see you standing at the door calling them in for dinner. The house smelling of fresh bread or baking."

"Little Jenny and Kayla remind me so much of our girls. Same sweet faces and that soft, dark hair. You used to grab that hair and pull it up in a handful on top of their heads and wrap a ribbon around it and call it a palm tree. The girls loved that. Then when they got older you brought it down into a ponytail. I can see them with that switch of soft hair streaming down their backs, sitting on the porch railing, telling tales to each other, and just watching the world go by. You used to yell at them for that. Couldn't tolerate idleness, could you?"

The old voice caught in a laugh that was half a cough.

"Caught hell for that all my life too, didn't I? Now you're gone there's nobody to get me outta my chair, bless your soul."

"It's good you never saw the house the way it is now. You loved the old place. Especially that veranda I built for you that went all across the front and down one side with the railing that stood high as my waist. And those pillars: those great, new, white pillars. They're not new anymore. The whole porch had started to sag last time I was by the place. But the kids sure loved to play on the rail, didn't they? Sure-footed as cats they were. A good place for kids. Except I never could figure why they hated the basement so. Remember when I'd lift the trap door and go down with 'em to show them it was safe? I'd take a small hand in each of mine and show them the shelves with the jars of preserves, the potato and apple bins, the coal pile. I think it was the coal bin that bothered them most."

The old man was quiet for a while. He knew it didn't matter if he spoke out loud or not but talking to his wife had always been the best way for him to clarify his own thoughts. His ideas glimmered and disappeared like fish in a stream if he didn't. He reached over and picked up the photograph on the bedside table. A round gentle face looked out at him from the frame. Chestnut hair and sparkling hazel eyes. A face he had known and loved all his life.

"Remember when you and I were little, Eliza? We weren't afraid of a coal shed. We weren't afraid of anything. A coal shed was a fascination; piled so high and dark in the back and sloping down to the single chunks in front, all blue-black and shining like the eyes of a thousand animals. The whole thing would grumble and shift when you took a scuttleful. The grandchildren would have liked the old place, eh?"

He emptied his cup and wiped his mouth on his sleeve then hoisted himself out of the chair and shuffled the few steps to the bed. Lying back on the bed on top of the quilt, he watched the twinkling of the Christmas lights around the window.

"Why do you suppose little Jenny was crying tonight? Did I upset her? Did I do something I shouldn't? You know I wouldn't hurt that little girl for the world. Remember those cigars she gave me that time? For no reason at all except she thought of me and knew I liked 'em? Course she was young and you had to help her...come to think of it now...was that Jenny?... or Kayla? That's sad. Somebody gave up their allowance for me and I can't remember. But I do remember sitting in the living room of that great old house of ours and blowing smoke rings with those cigars. I saw a little girl with an angel's face sittin' on the edge of each one as they floated to the ceiling."

He blew an imaginary smoke ring with trembling lips. Then a violent banging came from the hallway outside. He turned his head hopefully toward the door. He listened to the sounds of children thumping up the stairs and down the hall to their rooms to get ready for bed. Downstairs he could hear the soft strains of Christmas carols from the high tech music system in the living room. No one came in to speak to him. He sighed and turned back to the rainbow glow of the window.

"They should be sittin' around a blazin' fire and doin' their own singing. Too bad. Why don't people sing anymore, Liza? Is it because everything has to be done perfect? Done by pros or not at all? We used to sing all the time. It was one of the joys of being alive. Specially at Christmas. The one time of the year when magic shines in every heart, you used to say."

"But we'd sing any time, remember? Down by the lake we'd have those wiener roasts in the evening and sit around a fire singing anything anybody could remember the words to. Neighbours would see the flames and bring their lawn chairs down to join us. Then we'd bundle the kids in blankets and carry 'em up to the house. They'd be pretending to be asleep so they could get carried, you know, but we didn't care." He laughed and then hacked into a tissue.

Very softly his old voice rose again, drifting into the quiet corners of the room like the snow that still fell outside. "The lake…great place to raise kids. Swimming all summer. Riding the waves in to shore. Staying out way too long. Coming back to you with sunburn to have Noxzema cream smeared on hot little shoulders. I remember the smell of that cream…soft and hot from the sun. Smelled like the liniment we used to rub on horses down at the yard. Noisy family dinners around that big oak table Mike made for us."

Tom shook his head and blew his nose violently.

"Damn this is stupid! I'm not usually like this. Can't even think about those years tonight without blubbering. Never should have sold the old place. That's the way a man should grow old; workin' in the fresh air in his own garden and chattin' with the squirrels. Hell, they don't care if you're a senile old coot so long's you feed 'em."

He sighed and heaved himself up from the bed, dropped his robe on the floor and crawled under the covers. In the mirror on the opposite wall he could see an old man propped against several pillows. The glow from the bedside lamp drew patterns of shadow across a hairless skull. The mirror offered him a strange image of his head sitting atop two enormous lumps where his feet were. Odd place to put a mirror, he thought, directly across from the foot of the bed. A borrowed bed in his daughter's home. He no longer had a home.

The neat room with its stuffed bears and ruffled curtains wavered in his watery vision. There was another knock on the door…

"Grampa?" a timid voice said from the other side of the door. "Can I come in?"

"Oh Jenny. Of course, Honey. C'mon in." He heaved himself upright and wiped his face with the edge of the sheet.

A small, dark head, silhouetted in yellow from the hallway light, appeared in the doorway. He saw a foggy vision like a reversed candle flame. He fumbled for his thick glasses and wedged them onto his nose. The shadow focused itself into a small girl in a short, T-shirt gown that read 'I'm huggable'.

"I came to see if you were okay, Grampa. You were crying downstairs. I thought maybe you needed somebody to kiss it better. Would it help if I kissed you?"

"That would surely help, little one. A kiss from my favorite granddaughter always makes me feel terrific. C'mere. And give us a hug too since your nighty says I can."

She climbed up onto the bed bringing with her the smells of warmth, of love. Her tiny lips on his cheek were soft and wet as little starfish.

"Grampa? Did somebody do something mean to you tonight?"

"No, Honey. Why?"

"You cried. I saw you."

" Ah, yes. I was just missin' your Grandma tonight I guess." He settled back on the pillows with Jenny curled in his arms. He stroked the soft down of her hair with the back of his hand where the nerves still spoke to him without calluses. "I miss her most at Christmas. It's such a special, magic time." He paused. "And I guess I'm missing all the Christmases. The ones I've seen. And the ones I won't." He smiled down at her puzzled face. "It's okay, Pumpkin. It really is."

They sat quietly for a minute. The warm red of the Christmas lights shone in through the window chasing shadows from the room.

"Do you remember your Grandma?"

"No, Grampa," she replied.

"Will you remember me, do ya think?" he asked softly.

She twisted in his arms to look up at him to see if he were teasing her. Her eyes were dark butterflies newly opened.

"I don't have to, Grampa. You're here."

His breath caught in his throat and he coughed. The loneliness evaporated from his chest like mist from a lake.

"Yes, Pumpkin, You're right. At least for this Christmas I'm still here."

Publication Credits

Many of the stories in this collection have been previously published or broadcast. The author gratefully acknowledges the following:

The One-Eyed Chevrolet (Sept):
    CBC Alberta Anthology

Heartbeat on the Wind (Feb):
    CBC Alberta Anthology

The Boy Who Tried To Lose:
    Tyro Magazine

The Name of Morning (May):
    CBC Alberta Anthology and Calgary Writers Association Anthology

Silent Sky (July):
    CBC Alberta Anthology

The Day Summer Died (Sept):
    Prairie Journal Press

The Last Christmas (Dec):
    CBC Alberta Anthology

Other Books By This Author

Women Without Shadows

A collection of poetry exploring women's lives and their journey from living under the shadow of someone else to emerging from the shadows and into the light of their own strength. A slim volume of gentle and powerful poems, each poem telling a small story of its own.

Journey To Night Mountain

A delightful tale of self-discovery; a fantasy story in the tradition of Alice in Wonderland; a frolic through cultural references that will resonate with anyone who remembers the golden era of the 50's, 60's and 70's; and a touching story of friendship all wrapped up in the strange world of a future that we can only wish could come true.

Books can be ordered from the author at KathrynHartley.com

About The Author

Kathryn has had a life-long love affair with creative writing since she won her first poetry competition at age 10. She has published short stories and poetry in literary journals and anthologies over the years and produced a book of poetry: "Women Without Shadows". She has also published a YA novel: "Journey to Night Mountain". Her work, both short fiction and poetry, has also been featured frequently on CBC Radio's Alberta Anthology program.

Professionally she served as the Executive Director of the Calgary Region Arts Foundation for 23 years. Then she and her husband and son moved from Calgary to Nelson in search of a more natural life style surrounded by lakes to paddle, trails to walk, and mountains and valleys to explore.

In Nelson Kathy worked for the Nelson and District Arts Council for two years then retired to concentrate on writing and many volunteer positions. She lives with her husband and two Chihuahuas in the serene lakeside town nestled in the gentle green mountains of southern British Columbia.

Contact:
Email: cougarlake2021@gmail.com
Website: www.KathrynHartley.com